Welcome to Paradise

Welcome to Paradise

Twinkle Khanna

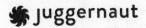
juggernaut

JUGGERNAUT BOOKS
C-I-128, First Floor, Sangam Vihar, Near Holi Chowk,
New Delhi 110080, India

First published by Juggernaut Books 2023

10 9 8 7 6 5 4 3 2 1

P-ISBN: 9789353451882
E-ISBN: 9789353451899

This is a work of fiction. Any resemblance to persons, living or dead,
or to actual incidents is purely coincidental.

Typeset in Adobe Caslon Pro by R. Ajith Kumar, Noida

Printed and bound in India by Replika Press Pvt. Ltd.

For Nani,
who can't read this book because she is dead
and may not have bothered to if she were alive.
We miss her.

Contents

The Man from the Garage

The cotton in Amma's nostrils matches the white in her hair. 'One should always be tip-top, Huma,' her mother would say when teased about dyeing her hair every two weeks. She would not want people to see her like this. Huma lights the incense sticks in her hand and places the holders around the refrigerated case that contains her mother's body.

The doorbell of their cramped apartment has been ringing all morning. This time, her brother is standing in the doorway. Huma had not been sure if Adil had received her messages from the hospital, if he was even in Mumbai. Her brother burrows his face into Huma's shoulder. Snot and tears rubbing against the thin cotton of her kurta.

'Huma, I can't believe she is gone. At least you all got a chance to talk to Amma, to say goodbye,' he says.

Chance. As if luck favoured Huma and she had won a lottery. Huma's eyes dart over him. It's an old habit. She takes in the eyes that always seem half closed. In the few photographs of the family together, Adil often looks as if he has blinked just as the flashbulbs have gone off. His curly hair, like the coils in a spring mattress, is flattened with water. He smells of sweat, musty clothes and something astringent – a hospital ward mixed with a boys' locker room.

Huma doesn't ask her brother why he has not returned her calls or where he has been. In the last three years, she has seen him less than half a dozen times. Adil follows her into the living room. He shrugs off his brown backpack and squats beside Amma's body.

Her mother's feet are pointed towards Huma. Small and delicate, they were the same size as hers. Each time Huma bought a new pair of shoes, Amma would ask, 'Are they comfortable?' Depending on the answer, Amma would slip them on. Huma can still see her walking across the room, kaftan flapping, her bent torso leading the way as she shuffled ahead in Huma's shoes.

Loss feels like the needle of a sewing machine – piercing through and lifting rhythmically; forgotten for a few moments, it slams down again. The salty Mumbai air heavy in Huma's lungs, as if it were liquid, going down the wrong pipe.

Huma had read about software programs that can mimic the departed. A facsimile of features, tones, frequently used sentences. She imagines feeding it videos – the one where Amma is handing Adil kheer with the smile she reserved for him. Or punching in memories – the time Raju, the cleaner, opened the bathroom door accidentally. Amma in a shower cap, enraged, stood there naked, yelling. Instead of covering herself with a towel, she started jumping up and down on the spot, as if there was an invisible skipping rope below her. Screaming at the boy. 'You want to see me, right? Have you seen enough?'

Huma wonders which version of Amma the program would generate.

She bends next to Adil. The white roots. Huma has bought her daughter a salwar kameez for the funeral, but Sara refuses to change out of her jeans. She will use Sara's dupatta. Drape it around Amma's face so the cowl covers her hair.

After an hour of serving tea to relatives she doesn't recognize, Sara is hiding in Huma's room with her cousin Saurabh. He is telling her about the time when Nani had picked them up from school. She had come to fetch them in her old jeep. 'She took off before I could even close the door. One leg was still out and then your grandmother said, "Hold on tight because I don't like using the brake or the horn!"' He laughs when he tells her this. She looks at his teeth. Even, white, all intact. She had punched him in the face once, in fourth or fifth grade. Broken a molar. She had been suspended from school. She can't recall what they fought about, just her arguing with her mother that it was a milk tooth and it would come back, and her mother locking her in a dark bathroom. It was Nani who opened the door and smuggled in ice cream to console her.

Her mother enters the room, her frizzy hair pulled into a bun and anchored with a pencil. 'That salwar kameez I got you, it's in my cupboard. I need the dupatta from that set right away,' Huma says.

Sara nods and adjusts her body, implying she is about to stand up, only to plop down when Huma turns towards the living room as someone calls out to her.

Sara had arrived last night from Mussoorie. At her boarding school, the seniors were allowed to keep their mobile phones, but seventh graders like her were only handed their phones on Sundays. Yesterday, despite it being a Thursday, she was given hers. Huma's voice had sounded hoarse as she said that Nani had passed away. It had started with a headache, her mother explained. They put her in an MRI machine and her grandmother got frightened because it was built like a coffin. She vomited. Choked on her vomit and that was it; it went into her lungs.

Now, Nani is lying flat on her back in the middle of the living room in what she feared the most, a coffin, a glass one, where they continue refilling ice to keep her body from decomposing. So that all the

5

people, who didn't come to see her grandmother when she was alive, have a chance to see her when she is dead.

~

In one corner of Huma's living room, uncles, aunts, cousins are debating over what to do with Amma's body. This is not a traditional approach, but her religious legacy is not what they consider regular either. Amma was born into an Ismaili Muslim family. Huma's father, who loved his sweet dal and his puja room with the silver idols that he polished every week, agreed to a conversion ceremony to placate Amma's parents. He was a funny man, her father. On Tuesdays, he would go to the temple and on Fridays he accompanied Amma to the jamaatkhana. To the people who questioned his all-encompassing beliefs, he would say, 'Religion is like a tree – it doesn't matter which one you choose to sleep under; they all provide shade.'

Huma remembers asking him, 'Daddy, tell the truth – you copied this tree bit from your Osho book, right?'

'Like me, my dialogues are also all original,' he had replied in Gujarati. When he passed away, he was cremated at the Shivaji Park Cemetery just as he had wished and without any of the fuss accompanying her mother's funeral.

In the noisy living room, the extended family has divided itself into two factions.

Team Crematorium, led by Padma Ben, Huma's father's sister, claims that, like Huma's father, Amma must also be cremated.

Team Cemetery includes the relatives from Amma's side. They argue that since she had spent her entire life following the Ismaili faith, she should be buried.

Murad, Amma's geriatric nephew, is holding court. He had once locked up his mother in her flat because she would not sign some legal documents. Each day, he would lower a basket with lunch and dinner from his apartment to his mother's bedroom window a floor below.

When Huma heard about the incident, she told Amma, 'That is terrible on Murad's part! He could have at least sent her breakfast too.'

Amma had looked at Huma with a blank

expression on her face before letting out a guttural laugh. 'Good joke, Huma,' she recalls her mother saying.

People don't remember commonplace things. They remember first times and rare occasions. Amma's compliments were seldom tossed in Huma's direction.

She watches them bicker, Padma Ben and Murad. *Burn. Bury.* Two words that differ by a single letter. She looks at her brother sitting beside Amma's body, ignoring the cacophony. She forgot about the dupatta. Sara. That girl, does she ever listen! Huma gets back on her feet and goes to her room. Sara and Saurabh are playing a game on Huma's iPad.

'Sara, what is wrong with you? I asked you to get that dupatta!'

'Your cupboard is locked,' her daughter says, 'What am I supposed to do? Break it down?'

⌒

Her mother tells her the keys are in the bedside drawer. Sara unlocks the cupboard and gets the dupatta. She is about to cross the living room to hand it to Huma when she sees *him*. His blue T-shirt and brown backpack stand out in a sea of white shirts and saris. *The man from the garage.*

It was during the summer break, a week after they moved in with her grandmother, when she discovered that someone was living in the garage at the other end of the compound.

The family would leave him food on an old oil drum outside the garage. One afternoon, Nani asked if she could lend him her comic books. Sara didn't know old people read comics too and he was at least thirty. But Nani insisted that Adil loved Superman and the X-Men.

Sara's comic books came back with bookmarks. These were not the slim, cardboard strips with cheery quotations. They were squares of silver foil. Burnt in places. Charcoal holes scattered across the shiny sheets. Her mother would examine the pieces of charred foil before throwing them away.

One monsoon, he went away with a Dr Mehta for a few weeks. When he returned, he moved into their apartment. As her Nani said, he did love comics. He told her he collected them. 'Marvel and DC both,' he said. Rare comics and first editions. He had stored them in cartons. One on top of the other, till they touched the ceiling. When she asked him where they were, he said, 'Sold them.'

He fixed a table tennis net across their yellow laminated dining table. After school, she would throw down her bag and challenge him to matches. He always won. This was before he started disappearing. He would be missing for a day or two and, on his return, he would sleep. Twelve to fourteen hours at a stretch.

The first time he hit her, she was asking Nani about clean towels. He charged up to her and said, 'Don't talk to my mother like this.'

Sara was wondering what she had said when he slapped her again. 'You bitch!' Sara called him. It was a term she had heard her mother use. She wasn't sure what it meant then but had known it was a bad word. She took off in fright, sprinting till she reached the end of the lane before realizing she didn't have any shoes on. Their watchman hurried down the lane and took her back home. Nani made her promise not to tell her mother. She said Huma didn't need more stress. Sara didn't tell her mother. Not even when her mother asked her why instead of Adil Uncle she had started referring to him as 'the man from the garage'.

One afternoon, when Sara was finishing her homework, she saw him heading towards the door with a camera in his hand. A toaster, a pair of earrings and a silver bowl had all gone missing recently.

Sara rushed after him, shouting, 'That is not yours!'

Curly hair tumbling over his forehead, he turned languidly towards her. Sara was ten by then, the tallest in her class, but he still loomed over her.

'You can't take it; you have to ask my mother first,' she said.

There was an instantaneous shift, as if someone had pulled his face in diametric directions. His eyebrows arched and his mouth stretched till Sara could see his lower teeth. He went into the kitchen and emerged with a large, grey-flecked grinding stone in his hand.

'Say sorry right now,' he said, raising the stone, levelling it with her jaw. She ran. Around the pillars of the living room, into her grandmother's bedroom where she was sitting with her embroidery hoop. Sara's hands were surprisingly steady as she locked the door. He began striking it with the grinding stone repeatedly. The door broke.

Nani pushed her against the wall, shielding Sara's body with her own as he stood before them.

11

'Say sorry right now! You think you are so smart! Let's see what happens to your head when I smash it.'

'Say it,' her grandmother whispered. Sara could feel the warmth of Nani's body against her chest, the dampness from the mouldy wall against her back. She shook her head.

Then she thought of what he had said. Smart. It was not the first time someone had used that term for her. Even amid overpowering fear, there was a flash of vanity. She imagined her head crushed. A dent as large as the stone on one side.

'Say it,' her grandmother repeated. Sara could feel her trembling. Her sour breath on Sara's face as Nani turned in her direction.

He swung the stone towards them. It hit her grandmother on the head. Sara sat on the floor, piss running down her leg.

'Sorry,' Sara said to the man who should have never been allowed to leave the garage.

Adil's head is bent as he adjusts the sheet over Amma's body, his hair spiralling over his face. Huma wants him to look up so that she can examine his pupils in the sunlight. She fights the urge to push up his long-sleeved T-shirt to check for track marks. When she first started seeing bruises on his arm, he told her he had developed diabetes.

When they had discussed Adil's addiction, she never told Amma that on all the occasions she had called his friends and driven around the city looking for him, she didn't blame him. She blamed Amma.

From the time they were kids, Amma had always taken Adil's side. After the drugs started, she remained in denial, giving him money repeatedly. When he returned Sara's comics with burnt foil stuck in the pages, Amma refused to believe he was back on heroin. Even when their helper told Huma that Adil had hit Amma, her mother, with a bandage wrapped around her head, insisted that she had slipped in the shower.

Sometimes Huma resented the attention, the love Amma reserved for Adil. Was it because he was the coveted son? Or does a mother always look out for her weaker child?

In their twenties, she had gone with him on a drive to look for his dealer. By then he had begun to talk about his habit, though he always said, 'I am not addicted, I am just dependent; there is a difference.'

As they drove through narrow lanes, he told her that it had started when he had taken the painkillers Amma had left in the drawer after her knee surgery. 'I took one and I never wanted that feeling to go.'

For a time, he had been a functioning user. He had a job in one of their uncle's steel factories and a girlfriend from the neighbouring building. This was before he started missing work, telling people he had been in car accidents when he wouldn't show up and, eventually, disappearing for months at a time. He would clean up but always go back to using. The withdrawal, he told her, felt like having food poisoning, malaria and fractured bones all at the same time.

Murad is using the living room couch as a podium as he drones on about taxes. He now claims that if he had a gun he would shoot all the ministers. His wife replies, 'The bullets would only hit me because you can't see properly, can you? All your life just giving big talks!'

He then directs his attention towards Adil. 'I know the mukhi at the Andheri jamaatkhana. I will call and tell him you are coming. You fix everything with him. With you, there is no problem, but I am warning you, Huma won't be allowed inside the jamaatkhana for your mother's prayer meetings.' Murad taps Huma on the back. 'Once you marry non-Ismailis, outsiders, the way you have, even if you are divorced from him now, we can't allow you in.'

Padma Ben immediately shuffles over to Murad and says, 'Who are you calling outsiders? You people are the outsiders! This is Hindustan – our country! There are many Muslim countries, you can go there. Go to the Gulf, go to Pakistan, who is stopping you?'

There was a time when both sides of Huma's family would gather to celebrate holidays together.

Then along came the burning train. In their Gujarat. Mobs went on a rampage. Over a thousand people were killed in the communal riots. The

15

aftermath transformed the dynamics within her family as well.

Huma feels a hand on her shoulder. Sara is standing by her side, her eyebrows pushed into a frown, holding a dupatta in her hand.

~

The man from the garage still has a dirty neck. Sara remembers watching Nani once clean his neck with a soapy washcloth and then use a cotton pad soaked in cologne to remove the accumulated dirt.

'How big Sara has become!' he says now and pinches her cheek.

Sara is used to people pinching her cheeks. The older relatives do it to all the kids. But when the man from the garage takes her flesh between his thumb and forefinger, kneading it for a moment, there is pain. Sara moves her head swiftly and sinks her teeth into his palm. He jerks his hand back, but she doesn't let go. Digging her teeth harder into his flesh. Till her mother yanks her away. She can see the indents of her teeth, a red semicircle on his hand.

Sara runs to her room and locks herself in. The

moment between the time he put his hand on her cheek and her biting him is dark. Maybe it has just become a habit – attacking before she gets attacked. The instant before she swings her arm or pushes her nails into someone's face is always blank, as if it didn't happen. Or like when she was reading *The Graveyard Book* and from page twenty-five she had gone to page twenty-nine, without realizing that the library book was missing a few pages.

Huma can sense neighbours, friends, all the relatives staring at her, at her brother, at her daughter rushing to her room. The crazy Shroffs. How many stories about Huma's family these people must have gathered over the years? Commiserating when her brother was again in rehab or when she returned home, divorced, with a child. And now they will talk about her daughter. The bite will not be forgotten. It will be discussed later when they are in their own homes. All secretly relieved that their children are better than the Shroffs.

She can see the marks on Adil's hand. It doesn't

leave her mind, the way Sara turned in his direction. Her teeth clamping down. Like the zombies in the movies Sara likes watching. They had seen the *Resident Evil* series together and Sara would keep pointing out plot holes. 'How can this be the scientist's flashback? She is not in the room, so how can they show what the zombie is doing inside?'

'Who are you and what are you?' Huma had asked her daughter, amazed at Sara's intelligence. All of thirteen and aware of perspectives.

'A future employee of Rotten Tomatoes,' Sara had replied with a broad smile.

She thought sending Sara to boarding school would change things, but her violent streak has not disappeared. Huma decides she will take Sara to a shrink and even those babas who brush people's heads with brooms to banish evil spirits. She will try everything. From medicine to miracles. But she will not do what Amma did. Huma will not let her child turn into a monster.

She can't talk to Sara now. She will do it once all these people leave. The extended family, after watching the matinee performance of 'The Crazy Shroffs' have gone back to their squabbling. The discussion has now deteriorated to which religion is superior based on which section eats beef and who eats pork. Murad finally brings up circumcision; he says, 'It is much more hygienic than what Hindus do.' This leaves Padma Ben speechless.

Huma wonders if her father would have found the whole episode amusing. His dead wife lying three feet away and the extended family quarrelling over pigs and penises.

~

It's been an hour since her brother left to meet the mukhi. Someone has ordered samosas and the family is sitting around the dining table as if they have dropped by for a Sunday meal. While chomping on his second samosa, Murad gets a call from the mukhi. 'Adil has not reached the jamaatkhana and they can't wait for him any longer,' he tells Huma with the phone clamped to his ear.

She imagines the sun cutting across the sky till it disappears into the west and Amma's body still lying in the middle of the living room.

'We have to go to the jamaatkhana ourselves, Murad Bhai, and sort this out. I want to be there for Amma's prayers.' Then Huma goads him with, 'Padma Ben is already talking to her pandit ji to come for the last rites at the Santacruz crematorium.'

On their way to the jamaatkhana, she breaks a red light and bribes the traffic cop with a hundred-rupee note. Huma drives away as Murad insists that it's too much and the policeman should give them fifty rupees back as change. She follows his directions till they reach a white building at the end of a dusty street.

The mukhi, a soft-spoken man, hears her out and says, 'We would not do this usually, but I remember hearing good things about your father. It is rare for a man to change his religion to his wife's. We can only allow you inside the jamaatkhana though, if you are willing to reconvert.'

Huma is asked to pay a small donation. She is then led to a table where she kneels on the ground as the mukhi's wife sprinkles water on her face. Huma is handed a white candy like she is a child waiting at the dentist's. She is moved to another low table, where a bearded man with a smattering of prayers informs Huma that her reconversion is complete. She is an Ismaili once again.

⌒

The van carrying her grandmother's body enters the cemetery gates. They lift her on to a stretcher and deposit her in a closed chamber attached to the pavilion. One family member is allowed inside to witness the body being prepared. Nobody volunteers.

Sara looks at her creased and rumpled mother standing at the other end of the pavilion. She wants to hold Huma's hand but is scared. Before leaving for the jamaatkhana, Huma had come to her room and said that Padma Ben would take Sara to the cemetery.

Sara tried talking to her mother. 'I didn't mean to do it, Ma. I got angry and it just happened.'

'You know, it's not just chickenpox and flu; uncontrollable anger is also a kind of illness. It can be fixed. But we will talk about this later,' Huma replied.

Sara doesn't look at it as an illness. She thinks it's

more like a full tube of toothpaste which squirts out with the smallest push, more than you intended and all over the sink.

In the crowded pavilion, an elderly aunt in a floral sari presses against Sara. She plugs a religious jukebox into a switchboard in front of Sara's chair. It has a picture of the Aga Khan that lights up and plays high-pitched chants. She then turns to Sara and says, 'Don't tell anybody, but when I went to pay my respects, I took some of your grandmother's hair. I will give you a few strands. You can put it inside a locket.'

When they open the chamber doors, Nani is lying on a raised marble platform in the middle of the room. People start moving around the platform, touching her grandmother's feet, crying, throwing flowers.

'It's difficult to lose a loved one, but she is in a better place now,' a man sitting behind her says. Lose. Like her Nani is a T-shirt that didn't come back from the laundry.

Standing on one side of the pavilion, Huma spots Sara sitting in a plastic chair and talking to a sari-clad relative. Sara should offer the elderly woman her chair, but her daughter doesn't move and is instead making strange faces at the old woman.

Amma's body is brought out. Huma touches her mother's hand. In all these years she has rarely seen Amma's hands lying still. She was always knitting, folding clothes, writing duas in lined notebooks. She squeezes her mother's stiff fingers and steps out to call her brother again. He doesn't answer. They are going to pick up the bier with Amma's body and take it to the burial spot. Heads covered, women are meant to watch from a distance. A son, the firstborn, must lead the way. In lieu of a son, the task is handed to the closest male relative. Daughters are not involved in these arrangements.

Cousins, uncles, family friends are now lifting the bier. Huma pushes her way to the front, hunching at first and then straightening when she finds a place for her shoulder under Amma's bier. Someone tries to stop her and she screams. They leave her alone. The crazy Shroffs. She walks with the men, chanting

23

till they reach the freshly dug grave. She helps them lower Amma's body into the ground. Her brother should be doing this. When Huma sees him, she wonders if he will say the same thing, 'At least you got a chance to say goodbye.' She throws the first handful of dirt on her mother's body.

When all the mourners leave, Huma walks to the freshly filled mound. She has a packet of fenugreek seeds. Amma would soak them overnight and consume them in the morning. Huma wants to plant them over Amma's grave. The smell of damp earth, of bruised petals, roses and tube roses fills her nose as she bends over Amma's grave. She sprinkles the seeds and Sara pours water from a plastic bottle over the loosened dirt.

When Sara was young, her grandmother would stop her from swallowing guava seeds. She would tell her that if she ate the seeds a tree would start growing inside her stomach, the branches coming out of her nostrils and her ears. It feels odd to think of plants sprouting out of her grandmother's body. But it still makes her feel better to think of Nani being present in some way, even as a patch of fenugreek, which Sara can come and see when she misses her too much.

Sara is sucking in her cheeks and blinking slowly. Huma recognizes that expression. It's when Sara is nervous or anxious. For a moment, she looks like the lost nine-year-old she had been when they first moved in with Amma. She doesn't know if Sara is what other people would call pretty, with her joint eyebrows and snub nose, but sometimes, when she looks at her daughter asleep by her side, she feels overwhelmed by how beautiful she is. The way your heart fills seeing the Golden Temple or the Taj Mahal. An object so majestic that, for a moment, it makes you forget all your grievances with the universe. Her phone beeps and she checks her texts. It is not from Adil. She messages him again.

Sara can see who her mother is texting. She knows he will not come. The same way she knows who took her mother's iPad and the speaker that was on the dining table this afternoon. She had watched him go into her mother's room, pace around the dining table. She had seen his brown backpack. Flat when he came in and full when he left.

Huma decides to wait for her brother. She remembers when he returned from rehab, the third or fourth time, he had hugged her and said that she was the person holding him together. Another afternoon, when the bathroom door was bolted and he wasn't answering, she had climbed in through the small window with the exhaust fan at the back. It was a tight fit even for her. He was lying still on the floor. A brown rubber tube tied around his arm. A syringe by his elbow. She unlocked the door, picked him up – he weighed less than her by then – and carried him out. She knows that she will have to carry him repeatedly and, unlike with Amma, there will be no one else to help.

Another half-hour, she tells Sara. Huma reaches for her daughter's hand as they sit on a bench under an old banyan tree. It's a relief to get out of the scorching sun.

Let's Pretend

Ranjit, unlike her, could charge a small fee as a professional wedding guest. The thought amuses Amita as she watches her husband making rounds of the banquet hall with his freshly shaved, florid cheeks. Not the pink of youth but the ruddiness that comes with broken veins and time.

Almost a decade ago, she had seen him across another banquet hall. A tall man, his face a buoy bobbing over wavy crowns. He circled the room, exchanging handshakes and business cards, till he stood before her, peering at the name tag pasted on to her blazer. Was it 2007? No, they moved to Leeds two years later, so it must have been around 2008.

'Amita,' he calls out now, striding towards her with a young man in tow.

'You remember I told you that I accidentally hit someone with an ice bucket yesterday? This is the poor chap. He has come all the way from Manchester for the wedding and will now be returning with a black eye.'

Amita can see the discoloration under the young man's left eye. She has seen him before, this man with a black eye and brown well-formed features.

Crossing the street? At a Starbucks? Her mind at a primitive level registering someone that belonged to her tribe. Race. An inconsequential factor till she moved here and began compiling a catalogue of small slights.

Ranjit adds, 'Manhar is originally from Bangalore.'

'Manhar?' Amita says. Louder than she intended. 'You lived in Shree building? Went to R.V. College?'

Manhar looks at Ranjit and back at her. 'I am sorry, but have we met before?'

'No,' she says, 'we have never met.'

Amita already regrets this brief conversation. What would it have taken to say something innocuous about the weather? 'Excuse me, I am going to get some fresh air,' she says.

Walking towards the banquet hall deck that overlooks Cromwell Lake, she wonders how she will explain this to her husband. A version of the truth? Or should she just tell him about Bangalore, beautiful men and, of course, Bua.

Bua would have found this entire exchange amusing. Amita imagines her aunt, a cocktail samosa in her hand, egging her along, 'Come on, Amita, let's go back and trouble him some more. Now you tell him you know he came first in the fifth grade.'

From the time she was a child, Amita had rarely seen Bua eat regular meals. It was either buttered pav, fries with curling edges or, as on the afternoon Amita had gone to ask her for a loan, a plate of yam, sliced and sprinkled with salt and chilli powder.

In her large bedroom, that overlooked Pune's Boat Club Road, Bua sat propped against two pillows. Her fingers and the corded mouse were both smeared with speckles of chilli as she played online poker. Amita rearranged the blanket over her aunt's wasted-away calves.

'It's good you got me into this online playing business,' her aunt said, turning back to the computer placed on a table across the rented hospital bed.

Amita had fifteen minutes. Once Bua's physiotherapist arrived, there would be no opportunity to talk.

'It's not the same as playing at the gymkhana, but it's easier to cheat,' Bua said.

'Less than an ace pair then fold,' she typed into the chat box on the screen, tagging a player called Sumit. She then replied to a Howdy66, 'Call Charlie's bluff!'

'Some of us have become friendly and we tell each other our cards. Better than wasting chips betting against each other. And look here – can you see my photo?' Bua asked.

Amita peered at the five players seated around a green table on the screen. Instead of her own photograph, Bua had uploaded a picture of Elizabeth Taylor from *Cleopatra*.

'I went to a fancy-dress party as Cleopatra once,' Bua said. 'I even had a dress specially made for it.'

'I remember Mama mentioning some costume party you had all gone to together.'

'Yes, your mother was there too. Dressed as a bride. Zero effort. Just wore her wedding outfit and made your father dress as a groom. Must have taken the clothes straight out of the trunk because they both smelled of mothballs. But what fun we had that evening! Let me tell you, pretending to be someone else gives you even more freedom to be yourself.'

Amita's mother had called it a scandalous evening. Bua had danced with a married man all night. Her mother seldom had any complimentary things to say about Bua. On shopping sprees, Bua used to buy shawls and embroidered pouches to give away as gifts. While often being the recipient of Bua's generosity, Amita's mother would later tell her that her aunt was 'showing off'.

Recalling Bua's continual kindness pushed Amita to mumble out her request for a loan.

'How much do you need? And for what? Is everything all right?'

She should just tell Bua. If anyone would understand it would be her. One of Amita's mortifying memories as a teenager involved stuffing socks into her cotton vest as her aunt barged into the room. The next afternoon, she was presented with a bra and instructions.

'Round and upwards,' Bua said. Fortunately, she performed the brisk massage for rapid growth on her own pendulous bosom instead of Amita's.

She heard Bua tell her mother, 'I feel so bad for her. Poor thing, flat as a bookmark.'

Her mother had chosen to take the remark as a personal affront instead of compassion. Amita's looks had been an intermittent cause of her mother's gloominess. While oiling her hair or buying her tubes of Fair & Lovely, she would throw in remarks like why Amita had taken after her father with his 'ordinary looks' and not her mother's side of the family, who were Konkanastha Brahmin women with pale skin and light eyes.

Amita's complexion, her breasts or the lack of them, had often bothered her, but it was after her relationship with Vikram had ended that she found it harder to ignore her flaws. She had always known that Vikram had been out of her league. She had put up with his comments about her accent, her legs, her breasts. But, after the breakup, his jibes were like burrs clinging to her skin.

Amita had tried padded bras but with unsatisfactory results. With the men she dated, it seemed to make things worse. She watched their faces when she undressed, the change in expression, as if they had ordered a main dish and been served an appetizer. A doctor had shown her the gelatinous balls that would jiggle under her skin. It scared her. The expense and the cutting and slicing involved in getting to a modest B cup. But she had decided to go ahead with it.

'What do you need it for?' Bua repeated.

Amita's leg was swinging of its own accord like she was kicking an invisible football repeatedly. 'I want to invest in a new bond scheme that has opened just this month,' she said.

'Bring out my chequebook, left drawer, and you can take your time to return it; there is no rush.'

When she returned with the chequebook, Bua asked, 'Should I play this hand? I have two tens.' She folded as soon as Sumit informed her that he had a flush.

'He is a good fellow, Sumit. He has given me his email address. I think I will write back, and we can be pen pals like back in the day.'

'Bua, you can't just give out your personal details online! You don't know what these people are really like.'

'They don't know what I am really like also,' her aunt said, 'and what is he going to do – it's an email address, not my house keys!'

When Amita continued protesting, Bua said, 'Ok, but what if I don't give my real details? You can make me a new email, like you made my old one?'

Amita, wanting to placate her aunt, created a new email ID. Swept away by Bua's enthusiasm, she found herself giggling as they debated over the right pseudonym till they both agreed on Reena Puri. Bua added that she was a thirty-seven-year-old, working in sales at a pharmaceutical company. A description that she seemed to have based largely on Amita.

~

Lately I have been thinking that the truth depends on your perspective. When standing on this planet, you know that clouds are above your head. But if you look at pictures of Earth in space and cut longitude lines through it, you will see oceans under your feet and clouds below the oceans.

'Isn't that nice? I never thought of it like that,' Bua said as she read aloud a snippet from Sumit's email. 'What should we write back?'

This had become a customary part of Amita's weekly visits – Bua reading out bits from Sumit's emails and then composing a reply.

With this email, his fifth or sixth, a picture was attached, as Bua, or rather Reena Puri, had requested repeatedly in the last few weeks.

A sturdy man in a checked shirt standing outside a glass building. A pen jutting out of his pocket and a laminated ID pass dangling from his neck. He was, well, beautiful. His face, carefully constructed, like angles had been calibrated, moulds made and recast before arriving at this interpretation.

Amita logged into Reena Puri's account from her computer that evening. She zoomed into the picture, examining the building ID pass, blurry letters that spelt his name at the top before descending into pixelated squiggles. His expression. Nose scrunched up over a broad smile, like he wanted to laugh at something but was struggling to stay still.

Bua, aside from commentary about television shows and poker games, often used Amita's anecdotes to build Reena Puri's fictitious world. Sometimes, when Sumit replied, it almost felt like he was writing to Amita.

In his next email, one she reread sitting in the dark, with a beer in her hand, he had written about listening to Kesarbai Kerkar's 'Jaat kahan ho' late at night.

Thirty years ago, they put a disc with musical compositions including this song on Voyager 1. I look up at the night sky and think that even if a large meteor causes our extinction, her voice and Raga Bhairavi will continue drifting between the stars.

There was nothing erotic about his views on mortality, music or meteors, but she felt a contraction of muscles between her legs. An awareness that narrowed from the room around her to the heaviness in her groin.

She locked the door. Enlarged Sumit's picture till it filled the screen. Unzipped her pants. Her fingers, pushing the beige underwear to the side. The guilt and embarrassment she felt a few minutes later lingered long after she washed her hands, scrubbing them, till they smelt of synthetic roses.

On a drizzly August morning, the senior manager, Aman Sharma, accompanied her on a sales visit to Bangalore. Amita had to ask Sharma to stow away her bulky bag in the overhead compartment. Her chest was still sore after the operation and the doctor had asked her to avoid lifting weights for another month.

After take-off, Sharma pulled out packets of snacks from his bag. Holding a greasy chip to her lips, he tried feeding her a bite. Though she was repulsed by this smarmy man sitting beside her, it was equally humiliating that she found his clumsy pass reassuring. At thirty-seven, when all her friends were married, Amita had recently told Bua that she felt like a packet of cold cuts coming close to the expiry date.

When she pushed Sharma's hand away for the second time, Amita laughed at herself. How could she feel reassured because Sharma was hitting on her? The office gossip had been clear: Sharma would hit on anything with two X chromosomes, even if she had a moustache thicker than his.

The next evening, Amita logged into Reena Puri's account. There was a new email with a photograph.

Sumit standing with a little boy, about ten or eleven. Both eating ice cream. The email stated: *You have told me so much about yourself and I apologize for not being as forthcoming. I have attached another picture. My wife passed away when he was five. My son, he is my North Star. And why do I talk about space so much? It's an occupational hazard.*

He worked at the Institute of Astrophysics he explained, in Bangalore, as a project engineer. The city she had visited the previous day. Would she have looked him up if she had known earlier? And on what pretext?

The following week, Amita arrived at Bua's for Ganesh Chaturthi. Bua was hoisted into the car and Amita sat beside her with the small idol of Lord Ganesha on her lap. Their car soon joined a procession of the elephant god's gigantic simulacrums, some two storeys tall on the back of trucks, all heading to Lakdi Pul to immerse their idols.

When Bua began chuckling about Sumit's last email, Amita diverted her attention to another section of the procession where people were dancing.

Bua's fabrications had been amusing at first, but now they troubled her. How would Sumit feel when he eventually discovered that he had been played by a seventy-year-old self-indulgent woman?

She had another Bangalore visit planned in five weeks. If Bua kept up this charade, Amita would tell Sumit the truth herself. She could write to him, ask him for his address. She could email him that she, or rather Reena Puri, wanted to send him something. Chocolates? No. Dry fruits? More plausible.

On the way back, Bua dismissed Amita's suggestion to end the correspondence. 'How is it harming anyone if I am pretending to be some Reena Puri? My body is pushed into stillness by this bloody Guillain-Barré, let my mind at least entertain itself. Come, Amita, hurry up and order some takeaway; I feel like eating Chinese tonight.'

⁓

It was November by the time Amita made her next trip to Bangalore. After her sales calls, she took a taxi to the address Sumit had emailed Reena Puri.

The building was rundown. A cockroach,

undisturbed and belly up, was the sole occupant of the lift. 'Use staircase' proclaimed a stained sign hanging from the grille. There were iron rods visible in the low ceiling, the edges of the steps uneven and crumbling all the way to the fifth floor. The discoloured bell emitted a piercing sound as Amita pushed it tentatively. She adjusted her blazer, ran her tongue over her teeth to erase lipstick stains.

In the still, dusty afternoon, there were no sounds of hurried feet or the clanging of unlatching bolts. She rang the bell again. The adjacent door opened. A heavyset woman in a printed nightdress, holding a Pomeranian, stood in the doorway.

'You want Sumit? He usually comes back by four,' she said. 'He should be here soon.'

Peering at Amita with raised eyebrows, she asked, 'You are a relative? Not from Bangalore?' The woman patted her dog as he barked at Amita and continued, 'I would remember if you had come before because he doesn't have many guests now. Not since his son went abroad. When Manhar was here, many youngsters would come, running between our two flats. Manhar and my daughter studied together you see, in R.V. College.'

She had seen a picture of Manhar. A broad-cheeked boy, in his yellow and navy school uniform. Abroad. College. Amita felt as if someone was asking her to multiply four-digit numbers in her head. She heard the lift whirring, the clanks and strains of metal and motor pushing against gravity.

'The lift – it is out of order, right?' she asked, a simpler question than the others whirling in her head.

'Oh no, Sumit should have told you. Don't tell me you walked up! The sign is there so that delivery people and servants don't use the lift. We tell all our guests beforehand,' she said, looking pleased with her ingenuity.

The lift halted on the fifth floor and an elderly man with faded eyes stepped out. He had a ring of hair running from one ear to the other. A bristly hedge safeguarding his bare scalp. It was the same man from the photograph she had enlarged, but much older. Closer to Bua's age. Lined, pouched and careworn.

'Oh, Sumit, you have a guest,' the neighbour said.

He looked at her expectantly. Amita, trying to reconcile the Sumit standing in front of her with the image she had been carrying in her head, was unable to speak. She felt a repugnance that made her hunch her shoulders and curl into herself. She had masturbated imagining her fingers as this man's.

In the dusty lift lobby, as Amita remained silent, Sumit asked, 'Yes? How can I help you?'

Bile rose in her throat. She tried swallowing it back down and felt like she was going to throw up. Unable to think of an answer, she said, 'Can I use the bathroom please? I am feeling a bit sick.'

He hesitated for a moment before he unlocked his door. 'Come in, the bathroom is to the left.'

Rinsing her mouth, Amita rubbed her face, steadying herself. She wanted to shake the old man. Demand answers. Threaten him with consequences.

When she stepped out of the bathroom, he was standing by the kitchen door, holding out a cup of tea. 'Have this, I have added extra sugar; it will make you feel better.' He had a deep voice, a careful, deliberate way of speaking. She took the cup from this frail man with trembling fingers.

'What's your name?' Sumit asked.

What would his reaction be if she said Reena Puri?

'Amita,' she said.

'You were waiting for me?' he asked, as she sipped her tea, trying to wash away the sour taste from her mouth.

Sumit's balcony had tomato vines, the way he had described in his letters. In the left corner, a desktop presided over the dining table. A sideboard was cluttered with photographs of Sumit and his son. In the array of photo frames, Amita could see Manhar growing till he was fractionally taller than his father. Sumit changed in them as well, incrementally, into the old man sitting across the table from her.

Recalling the neighbour's chatter, she said, 'I know Manhar from R.V. College. I was passing by and thought I would come and say hello. Is he here?'

'You didn't know? Manhar is in Manchester. He went after college to do his MBA. He is working in a large insurance firm there.'

The pride on his face was evident as he said, 'He has always been so bright. Right from the fifth standard he has always come first. In R.V. also, he used to top his batch but, of course, you would know that.'

Sumit continued talking about Manhar, switching between his schooldays and his son's recent engagement. Amita realized that in his emails he had been describing a world he had lost. The one he had inhabited when he was in his forties and raising his son.

'So, what do you do now,' she hesitated over what to call him, settling for, 'Uncle ji?'

'Not much any more. I have retired. But I keep myself occupied. I don't have access to telescopes any more, but I have my computer so I can still see pictures of galaxies and stars,' he said, gesturing towards the dining table. 'Manhar gifted it to me. He said, "We can write to each other every day, Papa. No more waiting for the post." He writes to me once or twice a month. In the UK, it's very busy, you must do everything yourself.'

An accordion of creases unfurled across his face as he smiled, fondness for his son mixed with the irony of the promise of instantaneous emails that seldom arrived.

'But it's all right, I have made some friends, mainly with other poker players online. They send me some emails so my inbox is not as empty as before.' He broke a biscuit in half, dunking it in the last dregs

44

of his tea. 'You didn't want to go abroad for further studies?'

She shook her head in response, watching him as he began picking up crumbs from the table and dropping them into the saucer. What was she going to say to this lonely man? Perhaps, if he had made suggestive remarks, she would feel justified in screaming at him. His letters had been about planets and plants. She was the one who had jumbled his words and created anagrams.

'It's good you stayed back. I wish Manhar had also gone for further studies somewhere in India. Sometimes I wonder if it's a mistake we parents make, sending them to a college in a foreign country from where they never return. University,' he said, drawing out the word, 'sorry, not college. Manhar used to always correct me.'

When it was time to leave, Sumit filled a small plastic container with dry fruits. She wondered if it was from the package she had sent. He handed it over.

'Take some,' he said. 'It was nice of you to sit for so long. It gave me a chance to do what all old men do, think about the past and bore young people like you with our stories.'

Old Hindi songs spill on to the banquet hall deck as the doors open and Ranjit brings her a drink from the bar. It's been a long day. They left home at noon to drive ten miles to the wedding venue. He asks her about Manhar.

'I will save it for the way back,' she says. 'It's entertaining so you won't fall asleep at the wheel.'

In the beginning, when she looked at Ranjit, she would sometimes feel like she had settled. Not settled down. Just settled. The way sediment falls to the bottom of a beaker. Thoughts like these still drift through her mind when someone comments on the eighteen-year age gap between them. But now they don't stick around long enough to bother her.

She wonders what Bua would have thought about Ranjit. She had never really taken to Vikram. After meeting him a few times, she recalled Bua saying, 'He is like a doughnut, all sweet-sweet on the surface, but I can see right through him.' Bua had the ability to see through most people. But not Sumit.

When Amita returned from Bangalore, she didn't tell her aunt that she had met him. Bua's physiotherapist had confided that, instead of being despondent at her lack of progress, Bua was in a cheerful mood because of the friends she had made.

Bua and Sumit – two lonely people presenting altered versions of themselves because they felt they would not be accepted in their present forms. Bua had said pretending to be someone else gives you more freedom to be yourself, but, perhaps, pretending to be someone else gives you respite from being yourself.

⁓

Bua passed away two days before Christmas. A heart attack. There had been no time for her to take the Sorbitrate she kept as an emergency measure.

A few weeks later, Amita mustered the courage to go through her aunt's belongings. Segregating old kaftans and never-worn leggings. The hospital bed had been returned. The room was empty aside from a trolley and the computer blinking away.

Amita switched it on. Bua had a few minimized windows. The poker website and her email accounts.

Some spam, a few emails from her friends and four from Sumit. She emptied the hard drive and gave the computer to their helper's son.

That evening, her eyes swollen with grief and dust allergies, Amita wondered if she should tell Sumit about Bua's death. Inform him that his friend, the one who looked out for him through glitchy connections and across two-dimensional card tables, did not exist any more. In any form. Where would she begin? Or should she just leave it alone? He would eventually stop writing.

She thought of Sumit's extra-sweetened tea, the container with dry fruits. She could see him, an old man in his empty flat looking at his empty inbox.

Bua with her poker and her Reena Puri charade had been joyful till the end. And Sumit? Wasn't he living according to what he had said in one of his emails? *Contentment is about cooperating with life, it's about acceptance.* Two people who had kept their spirits up despite their circumstances. It was Amita who had been the most dissatisfied out of the three.

She logged into Reena Puri's email account from her own computer. *Sorry,* she typed, *I couldn't write earlier. A close relative passed away recently.*

⁓

Ranjit tells her about a woman who was stuffing snacks from the buffet table into her bag. She leans against her husband watching Cromwell Lake's clear waters deepen into a crinkled navy as the sun sets.

When she met Ranjit, almost two years after Bua passed away, she didn't follow her usual pattern. She still wasn't sure how it had begun in the first place. The need to pursue men based on symmetrical features and broad shoulders. Vikram and the ones before him. Men who, as it turned out, had never been particularly nice to her.

By the time she started dating Ranjit, she had given up on the notion that larger breasts or a certain kind of man would make her happy. Or maybe she had just grown tired of being alone. With Ranjit, she waited till she got past the grey strands on his chest and his plain features. During sex, she would close her eyes at first to stop herself from drying up, asking him to use his tongue.

It was gradual, her getting drawn to him. She could never pinpoint the exact day she found herself absorbed in his ready smile, the one that made people gravitate towards him. Though Amita teased him repeatedly with 'I have never met anyone who doesn't like you. How are you conning all these people?', she knew he was incapable of affectation. It would never occur to him to be anything but himself.

When she told Ranjit about her surgery, she had been comfortable enough to joke about it. 'After I die, my breasts will remain intact over my decomposing body. You can come to my grave and visit them if you miss me too much.' They laughed as they began making up scenarios about her immortal breasts till he said, 'But you know, it's more likely that I will go first.'

Her husband is pointing out the stray guests who have escaped the party and are sitting on the dock below when Manhar comes up to them.

'Excuse me, but I must ask you, how do you know so much about me?' he says.

What were the chances that, after all these years, she would bump into Manhar at Ranjit's nephew's wedding? But it shouldn't shock her; after moving here, she realized that all the Indians tended to flock together. Everyone knew someone's cousin, brother, mother-in-law. Packets of spices and vegetables that didn't have English names were ferried from one family to another.

'Your father,' she says, 'we used to play poker together; he would mention you all the time.' She had continued exchanging emails with Sumit for almost a year till he stopped replying.

'Oh, you know Papa! He is in Manchester with us now,' Manhar says. 'After we had Anya, it was better to have family around to keep an eye on things. And, yes, he loves poker. Just between us, my wife complains about all the poker nights he arranges at our place, but Papa and I outvote her.'

When the emails stopped, she thought, like Bua, he had also passed away. She pictures him now, walking his granddaughter to school, having tea with his son, playing poker around a dining table.

'Sorry, your name is Amita, right? I will tell Papa. He will be happy to know I met you.'

'Not Amita. Tell him you met Reena,' she says as her husband looks on, questions and puzzled amusement lighting up his face. 'It's my pet name.'

Nearly Departed

Dear Chief Justice,
I hope you are in good health. My name is Madhura Desai
and I am an eighty-six-year-old retired schoolteacher. I
have a petition that I would like to present to you. Being
of sound mind and without any external pressure, I want
to avail myself of a fundamental right, one overlooked
in the Constitution – the right to die. I am seeking
permission for active euthanasia, a hospital-assisted
suicide.

I have been diagnosed with Parkinson's and I have
recently suffered what, in layman's terms, is called a
ministroke. I am aware that this is not a terminal disease,

53

but the road ahead is clear. Before it progresses to the point where I become a burden, it would be better to end this journey at a time of my choosing.

At my age, she added, and then, recalling that the chief justice was nearly eighty, amended it. *At our age, how many years do we have left and what lies ahead aside from illness and suffering? In fact, my advice to you would also be to follow the same path. Not right away, of course, but perhaps when you reach eighty-five. It is a nice cut-off age.*

She considered deleting the last paragraph. What if the chief justice was offended by this reminder of his own mortality? Well, she was merely laying down the facts.

If truly life must be preserved at all costs, then we would not have capital punishment or slaughter other living creatures with such detachment. Life has meaning, even among lesser creatures, only when they have utility.

I am writing to you with the hope that you will grant my plea. Please consider this an urgent matter. Time is not on either of our sides.

Warm regards,
Madhura Desai

The dogs of Tilak Road had learnt a new trick. They had started sleeping on top of the parked cars lining the street. A strategy that saved them from turning into roadkill. Under the full moon, as Madhura watched, one clambered onto the roof of a red Maruti. Neck extended, with ears upright, he surveyed the rest of his pack.

Her weak bladder and the recent requirement for a walker had changed her into a restless sleeper. Unaccustomed to the walker's rolling, shuffling rhythm, she found herself wide awake after her bathroom visits. Or it could just be Parkinson's giving her yet another gift. Insomnia, she had read, was a common occurrence.

She sat in the dark, sipping her tea, wondering how long she would have to continue this nightly vigil. In the five weeks since she had sent her plea, she had not received as much as an acknowledgement. She had written to a few NGOs, attaching the emails she had sent to various government leaders, but even they had not replied.

Two strays leapt off bonnets and began chasing a passing cyclist with a volley of barks. She watched them race down the lane till they disappeared around the corner. At least she had something to look out at unlike the flat below her's that faced the compound wall.

～

It had been raining all July, but that afternoon the taps ran dry. This was a recurring event. Madhura was prepared with a half-filled bucket in the kitchen. She was using her stored water to wash a few slippery tomatoes when the doorbell rang. Tai must have forgotten her key again. And she was late. Madhura wiped her hands, gripped the walker securely and made her way to the door. She would have to talk to Tai about her irregular schedule. Hired as a temporary helper after Madhura's fall, Tai – without either woman broaching the topic – had continued working for her.

Instead, on her doorstep, brandishing a mike, stood a reporter with a cameraman in tow. After verifying her name, the reporter stated that he had seen her plea posted by someone who worked at the Gita Kidney Foundation. He then turned to the camera and said, 'This is Prakash Dwivedi and here is News

Now's exclusive report on the teacher who wants to kill herself! She has sent emails seeking permission from the prime minister's office, the Supreme Court and, shockingly, has even advised the chief justice of India to commit suicide!'

Madhura tried telling the reporter that she had not permitted anyone to make her plea public. Still, the reporter, in a loud and excitable voice, continued, 'This is the state of our grandparents today. This is how Western culture has influenced us! Children abandoning their old parents, leaving them with nothing to look forward to except death.'

He then began quoting parts of her emails, all out of context. Over the last few years, she had observed news anchors adopting a dramatized, almost parodic method of presentation, but this was ridiculous.

'Madhura ji, why have you written all these emails? Is it to get attention? Or do you really believe that the elderly don't have a place in society?' the reporter asked.

This boy was either dense or, more likely, deliberately misconstruing her words. 'Of course, senior citizens have an important place in society, but just the way we have the right to live, should we not have the right to die? And, tell me, if I don't write to our government heads, then what should I do? Should I put out a Facebook post requesting kind strangers to come and kill me?'

Her tremors started bothering her. She could sense the small involuntary movements of her fingers, back and forth, like she was trying to adjust a radio knob to find the right station. 'Please excuse me now, I have to prepare my lunch.'

Dwivedi thrust his mike back towards her, 'Madhura ji, you seem so sharp and alert for your age – do you have any diet tips you can share with our viewers that have helped you stay this way? Tell us, for example, what will you have for lunch today?'

'Mr Dwivedi, since you have already helped scramble my brain this afternoon, I will make some toast to go with it,' Madhura called out over her shoulder as she turned back towards the door.

Tai arrived an hour later with her orchestra of clattering bangles, lovelorn ringer tunes and chiming anklets. Her face was drawn. 'Memsaab, Jitu said some news people had come here? What did they want?' she asked in her customary mix of Marathi and Hindi.

'Nothing important.'

Madhura didn't look up from the chopping board she had laid out on the dining table. Despite her trembling hands, she sliced the onion into symmetrical pungent rings, dividing the thick core into four pieces.

'I already know,' Tai said. 'They interviewed Jitu too.'

Learning that the watchman had been the subject of Dwivedi's exuberant reportage made her queasy. Her interactions with Jitu had been minimal till the accident. He had broken her door down though, and accompanied her to the hospital. She could imagine the reporter egging him on to get all the gory details.

'Memsaab, God has given us this life and it is His to take away. If it was your time, you would have reached heaven, not the hospital. You can't interfere with God's will.'

Madhura did not argue with her. She had noticed that those hard done by fate needed to believe in it the most. When Madhura didn't respond, Tai, assuming it was a signal to continue, made another declaration. 'Also, don't mind me saying it, but when I first saw a programme where that Rakhi Sawant said that ceiling fans should be banned so people can't commit suicide by hanging from them, I told my husband she was completely mad. But now I am praying that you don't get such ideas. I heard some young girl in Bhayandar tried to hang herself from the fan and the ceiling came crashing down. Let me tell you, your ceiling is also very weak. Whenever I am dusting, half the plaster falls off, so please don't try all this; you will fall and break your other leg also.'

They both looked up at the swirling fan, the blades darkened with grime along the edges.

Tai, rubbing her fingers across her wide mouth, said, 'I will get the stool.'

'To remove it?' Madhura asked.

Her eyes darted sheepishly towards Madhura and back to the fan.

'No, to clean it. I forgot to do it last month.'

Madhura made her debut on television that weekend. She was alerted of this development by a phone call. She shook her head as the name 'Pipi' flashed on her phone. The pet name always took her back to the summers of their youth in Surat. Pipi was often teased by the other boys over the moniker chosen by his parents to shorten the grandstanding Padmakant. Wielding her grandmother's stick, she had once chased after the bullies when she discovered a crying Pipi in the front courtyard.

It was not him calling, of course. Over the last two years, every few months, on birthdays and Diwali, his daughter-in-law Sharda had started calling from Pipi's phone. Madhura would sometimes hear Pipi in the background, murmuring in Gujarati. A polyglot who had forgotten all languages aside from the one of their shared childhood.

'Is Pipi all right?' she asked. The unexpected call was making her anxious.

'Yes, he is fine,' Sharda replied in an impatient tone. 'But what is this? It hurts to hear you say such things. What will everyone think? That we are the type of people to abandon our relatives like this?'

'What are you talking about, Sharda?'

'We saw you on TV. You said you want to die and want to put out Facebook posts asking strangers to kill you.'

'When did all this come out?' Madhura asked.

'Some idiotic reporter had come here, but I didn't think anyone would bother putting the nonsense he was saying on the news.'

'We all saw it yesterday. First, they were talking about a man who has been in a coma for decades and how the court isn't giving permission to let his family remove the ventilator, and then they had your part. Even my father-in-law was very upset seeing it.'

Considering Pipi could barely comprehend when he needed to use the bathroom, Madhura found it hard to believe he had registered her presence on a flickering screen.

'Taking your own life is a sin,' Sharda added. 'You know what the Vedas say about it, right? And you must also be aware that people who end their own lives are not reincarnated; they just turn into ghosts.'

A ghost. In all her contemplations of what lay on the other side, Madhura had not factored in this possibility. It was an amusing proposition.

'Don't worry, Sharda. Surat is very far away, and I have never heard of ghosts taking trains to go and haunt people. So you are completely safe.'

'Everything is not a joke, Madhura Ben.'

'Madhura Ben' is what Pipi would also use to introduce her to people when he took her on Sundays to the Mahalaxmi Racecourse. In Gujarati, 'Ben', along with being a sign of respect, meant sister or cousin. Her aunt's sister-in-law had married Pipi's uncle. But it suited him to let people think they were closely related. Sometimes he even used the word cousin when he referred to her in front of acquaintances.

If Madhura did not get her off the subject, Sharda would drone on for the next hour. 'Tell me about Raju. What is he doing now?'

Till Pipi's condition deteriorated, there had been an established routine. He would come to Bombay every few weeks to check on his rental properties. Sometimes Raju used to accompany his grandfather. The duo would come to Tilak Road straight from the station with vada pav and green chillies wrapped in greasy newspaper. They would sit around her dining table, the smell of fried potatoes and masala tea intermingling with the boy's excited chatter.

'I don't know what to say . . . Raju quit his job, left Bangalore and is now coming to your Bombay. I was going to call you earlier and tell you, but looking after my father-in-law takes so much out of me that I just forgot.'

Madhura knew Pipi needed constant care, and, with Sharda's husband working in Dubai and her son leaving Surat, Pipi had become her sole responsibility. Despite Sharda's sometimes abrasive personality, she empathized with her. Having spent years caring for her father, Madhura was familiar with the world of bedpans and bone-deep weariness.

'What do you think, Madhura Ben?' Sharda repeated, forcing her attention back to their conversation.

'About what?'

'This film business! Raju doesn't want to do his website work any more. Now he has a job as an assistant to some director. His grandfather is also very upset with him.'

Once again Pipi had been thrown in to strengthen Sharda's claims, the way cereal boxes were gussied up with declarations of fortified vitamins and minerals these days.

'When Raju comes to meet you, please put some sense in his head. Tell him to come back to Surat and forget about all these silly things.'

After Sharda disconnected the call, Madhura continued sitting in the rattan chair facing the window. They were putting up a new billboard across the street. The last one with a model drinking some cola had collapsed in the previous week's heavy rain. Her ceiling had leaked too. It did every year, in the left corner by the window. Pipi used to joke that she could install a bathtub under it.

During one episode of torrential monsoon rains, they sat by the window and watched people wading in waist-high water. The city was flooded and Pipi's train back to Surat had been cancelled. She put a bucket under her dripping ceiling and made hot cups of tea. They were both in their seventies by then and Pipi had already started losing names, the way people misplaced keys and spectacles. She could see him hunting for them, with blank frightened eyes and a still mouth. He said it happened only when he was tired or hadn't slept enough.

That night, mid-conversation, he asked her, 'You remember when he told me to put all my money on that one horse? What was his name?'

'The horse's name?' she asked.

'No, that chap – you know – my friend.' He

stopped and then added, 'The one with the glasses-shasses.'

'You mean Genius?'

'Yes, Genius! Because of him, I bet five thousand rupees and it was all gone in less than ten minutes.'

Genius used to work for Turf Works. They printed race cards with details of every race across multiple centres. Pipi and he would sit for hours with their blue-and-white booklets. When Pipi would lose after getting a tip from Genius, he would curse his friend. 'You are as far from a genius as scotch is from urine,' he had once told Genius as they sat in her living room after a bad day at the races.

The first time he introduced her to Genius, he had said, 'Madhura Ben makes graphs of each horse's derby wins.'

And she did, for over three decades. Pipi wanted the charts made and he claimed she was better at mathematics than him. It was the truth. Right from the time they were in school, till her family moved to Bombay after her tenth-grade exams, she had always helped him with his maths lessons.

One evening, after she had done Pipi's homework for him, they continued sitting in their abandoned eighth-grade classroom, talking away, the smell of chalk merging with that of his hair oil. Their arms were folded over a wooden desk decorated with scratched initials and romantic declarations.

She finally asked, 'What time is it? I don't want to be late for dinner.'

'Even I don't want to be late. There is going to be pink custard today.' He said it without a trace of irony. His mother's attempts to be modern didn't just stop at hiring an Anglo-Indian woman to tutor her son in conversational English. She also attempted making puddings. Pipi's enthusiasm for indulgences even encompassed these bowls of custard, the colour and flavour of antibiotic syrup unmitigated by the occasional chunk of a banana or the sliver of an apple.

They hurried out of the classroom and reached the main door. It was locked. Pipi pushed against it a few times and said, 'We can jump out from the back window.'

He climbed out of the window and, with a small leap, he was standing on the muddy school grounds looking up at Madhura.

'I can't jump,' she said.

'It's not difficult. I will catch you.'

She sat on the window ledge and lowered her hips tentatively, an inch at a time, till he had his arms wrapped around her thighs.

Madhura let go. She slid till their foreheads were aligned and he gripped her waist. His nose pushing against her spectacles, her feet still six inches above the ground. Falling in love, she noted, in the most literal way possible.

Madhura, using the chair for support, tried reaching for her walker and knocked over her phone from the armrest. When she bent to pick it up, she was distracted by the sight of her hands. Thickened veins like bumpy, uneven seams shoved under the skin. And those fingers, those jittery, undisciplined fingers—soldiers refusing to obey commands, fidgeting when they were meant to stand to attention. She picked up the phone and dropped it again.

Then Madhura had, what she called, a bout of emotional incontinence. She first startled herself with a fit of laughter and then she cried. Her doctor said it was a common occurrence after a ministroke. He said it happened to people who had Parkinson's. He sometimes said that Parkinson's caused the stroke and sometimes that Parkinson's could be due to the stroke. Her diagnosis was like an Agatha Christie novel. The husband did it. The butler did it. The gardener did it. Except, she wasn't sure if they would know even at the end.

At least Pipi had a clear diagnosis. Alzheimer's, they said. Eventually, Pipi could not manage the train journey to Bombay that he had taken for over forty years.

Initially, she used to go down to Surat to see him. It drained her to perch on the plastic chair by his bedside, month after month, watching his personality evaporate like a beaker filled with isopropyl alcohol in a lab experiment.

What is life without a purpose, without something to look forward to, without someone who needs you? What did she have ahead aside from becoming like her Pipi?

From her kitchen window, Madhura could see her neighbours stringing a rope with a decorated clay pot for the Janmashtami celebrations. The little girl and her mother next door were also participating. It was good that they were getting to know people. Tai, who seemed to prefer gossiping to cleaning, had already informed Madhura that the family had moved here from Lucknow.

They were hoisting the pot high up across the lane. The following day, regardless of the rain, the neighbourhood boys would gather to make a human pyramid. They would climb on each other's shoulders, slip down and scramble back up, till they finally reached the top and cracked the pot open with a stone.

She contemplated asking Tai to bring a chair into the kitchen before she left for the day. Tai wouldn't come to work on Janmashtami and if Madhura wanted to sit by the kitchen window, it would be difficult for her to drag in a chair while balancing on her walker.

The doorbell rang and then the main door squeaked open. Voices drifted into the kitchen. One, she recognized as Tai's and, the other, a stranger with strongly accented Hindi, was replying, 'Yes, chai will do. No sugar.'

Wondering whom Tai had let loose inside her house, she made her way into the living room with an exploratory, 'Yes, can I help you?'

A plump woman in a knee-length dress turned towards her. She wore a string of pearls on her neck and had short hair, perfectly curled into a half halo that looked like a ficus hedge trimmed by a topiarist.

'Mrs Bharucha,' she introduced herself with a determined smile and added, 'let's sit at that small table, shall we? It will be easier to set up.'

Tai, who had shooed away a few reporters over the last couple of days, had clearly crumbled in front of her well-groomed visitor's tenacity.

'Interesting choice of music,' Mrs Bharucha commented as 'We Are the Champions' continued streaming from Madhura's bulky computer.

She usually had music playing through the afternoon, putting it on at exactly three o'clock. It conformed to the structure of her jotted-down schedule. Pencil lines that cut through the day, carving it into manageable pieces. Thirty minutes blocked for reading the paper. The next hour was marked Chess. Five in the evening was saved for tea with a single Marie biscuit. Each hour demarcated from the next, while the days all blurred into one.

'Queen, isn't it?' Without waiting for a confirmation, Mrs Bharucha continued, 'Freddie

Mercury, he was also a Parsi you know. My uncle Peroz knew his parents well. What was his real name? It's on the tip of my tongue and now it will annoy me till I remember.'

'Farrokh Bulsara,' Madhura said.

'Ah, sharp memory! I am terrible at remembering trivia. But good, yes, this is very encouraging. Can we switch it off, though? It's a bit distracting.'

Mrs Bharucha was not a journalist, though she asked questions in a similar probing manner.

'I am, what some people would say, an activist, but, really, social worker is how I look at myself.'

She worked with Clear Aid Foundation, she explained, and had tracked Madhura down after seeing a debate over her plea on an online platform. Mrs Bharucha pulled an iPad out of her cavernous handbag. Propping it on the table, she put on the programme-bickering panellists intercut with clips of Madhura's conversation with Dwivedi.

At first, Madhura found it difficult to identify with the woman she saw in the video. In the last decade, mirrors had been largely used to focus on precise features. An eye with a trapped eyelash or a boil next to her nose. It was startling to realize that this old woman on the screen, with skin that appeared to have been folded multiple times and then redraped over her bones, was really her. Always diminutive, age had further narrowed down her dimensions and whittled down her eyebrows till they were shadowy outlines peering over the top of her brown spectacles. She shook her head ruefully as Mrs Bharucha, lifting Tai's milky cup of tea, said, 'It is an interesting premise. We can really do something with this, Mrs Desai.'

'Not Mrs,' Madhura said with a smile, 'but you can call me Master Desai if you like. A master's in Life Science does legitimize the use of that title.' This was a frequently repeated quip from the days when she had to gently correct people about her marital status. Receiving a particularly vacant stare, she added, 'Just Madhura is fine.'

Mrs Bharucha, in turn, did not offer the use of her first name. She had another sip of tea and then said, 'Can I ask you a personal question though? Why haven't you thought of dying by suicide instead?'

'I have looked into it. But the odds are against me,' Madhura replied. 'Forty per cent of those who attempt suicide, fail. If I miscalculate, then either I will end up suffering for an indefinite period before dying, or worse, I will survive.'

'Yes, you have a reasonable argument there. As I was saying earlier, this is an opportune moment. You have already garnered some attention and we should capitalize on this right away! Have the government agencies replied to your plea? From what I have gathered, they are merely going to pass it on from department to department till it is lost in a paper shuffle. Well, that is unless we raise our voices and compel them to give in to our demands.'

Mrs Bharucha had a plan. One that would not leave the elderly languishing. She claimed she would save Madhura and others like her from botched attempts at suicide. Her printed dress rustled as she moved her hands expansively. There was a steadiness to her voice, a confidence in her manner, that Madhura found comforting, if slightly intimidating. Mrs Bharucha pulled out a notebook and started making lists. She said there were interviews to be scheduled, protests organized, politicians persuaded, polls tabulated and even a peaceful march could be coordinated outside Rashtrapati Bhavan.

She continued telling Madhura how she had once tied herself to a tree at the Aarey Milk Colony protest for eleven hours. Didn't she have to urinate at some point? Madhura wondered, while admiring her determination.

'And do you really have other alternatives aside from waiting endlessly for a response from the government?' Mrs Bharucha asked at the end of her pitch.

~

The curd rice lay untouched as Madhura sat by the table that evening. Dusk crept in through the windows. She had spent the last half-hour sitting in the dark, thinking about Mrs Bharucha's points. She was right about one thing, that woman – the endless delay. It was already August and Madhura didn't know how much longer she was willing to wait.

Slowly, she cautioned herself as she got to her feet. 'Don't pivot but take a U-turn,' the doctor had told her, like she was guiding the steering wheel of a car instead of her walker.

Familiar sounds drifted in through her kitchen window as she put the food away in the fridge and started washing her plate and the small pressure cooker. Blaring televisions, a child crying, someone from the floor below practising on a harmonium.

The windows had been closed the day of her fall all the way back in January. The bowl in her hand had tumbled first. Cracked white ceramic, spilling the soaked lentils. A sinking sensation in her limbs. Her foot folding under her as if it was made of dough.

When her eyes opened, she assumed she had been asleep in her bed and had wondered why her mattress felt rigid and cold against her back. There was no pain at first. Then it had bounded up, digging its throbbing claws into her flesh. Holding on to the table legs for support, she had attempted to hoist herself upright. Up and back down. Her left side, from her foot through her hip, held in a lacerating grip that tightened with every movement.

A spider had appeared. Had it been there that evening or the one after that? On the peeling wall above the kitchen door. Crossopriza something, she could not recall the complete nomenclature. She had tracked the spider's movements, imagining it looking back at her with its eight eyes.

She had lain on her tiled floor for four days. Unable to move. Covered in her own waste and convinced she would only be discovered when the stench of her decaying body trespassed into the building corridor.

⟡

Raju showed up on an overcast afternoon later that August with muddy shoes and a jar in his damp hands. 'Madhura Aunty, I don't know if you remember, but you taught me how to make this pickle.'

Madhura carefully placed the glass jar with the strips of turmeric, ginger and sliced chilli floating in lemon juice on the dining table. She didn't recall teaching the boy but there had been a time when the turmeric pickle had been a staple in her kitchen.

Raju slipped into her life with an easy familiarity. Madhura wasn't certain if he was lonely, or if she, like the applique bag with Kathi embroidery he usually carried, was a reminder of his past. Breaks between production schedules had him lazing on her divan, watching old movies. She didn't know why Sharda had been taken aback by her son's desire to become a director. For as long as Madhura could remember, Raju had always been a film buff.

In the late nineties, Pipi would sometimes leave Raju with her as he went off on his rounds. They would usually go to Chandan Cinema for the matinee show.

'They had the best popcorn you used to say,' Madhura remarked, recalling the smell of butter and salt overpowering the occasional waft from dank armpits from the neighbouring seats.

She had a picture of one of their expeditions. On Raju's insistence, they pulled it out from the dented tin box shoved on top of her closet. The dust made her throat itch as soon as the lid was off.

'You look just the same,' Raju said, peering at the photograph of the two of them standing together in a ticket queue. Pipi had bought Raju a camera on that trip and the boy had taken over a dozen pictures that day.

'Which means I looked all of eighty-six even when I was a young sixty-seven? That's rude,' she teased Raju.

'No, no, I didn't mean to be rude-shud. I was just saying you look as nice now as you did then.'

He had a funny way of speaking. Like his grandfather. Both had a habit of using rhyming words. 'I am going for a quick walk-shalk,' Pipi would say, or 'Have a bath-vath and we will leave.'

She examined the photograph closely. Raju with a pinwheel in one hand was smiling for the camera. A broad grin with his two front teeth pressing onto his bottom lip, and with so much oil in his hair that it looked like a family of slugs had colonized his scalp. She was standing half a step behind him, her hand on his shoulder, with a smile that matched his in width. This was years before Pipi's diagnosis.

She felt a sense of comfort in Raju's frequent visits. Lanky as a teenager, he was now over six feet tall and still had a slight hunch – one that he straightened out periodically before immediately slouching down again. He had started looking more like Pipi. There was something about his eyes, the shape or the expression she wasn't quite sure, that was reminiscent of his grandfather's.

That evening, Tilak Road turned into a muddy stream as rainwater overwhelmed the clogged drains. Madhura could see the dogs huddling in doorways to get away from the flooded street. Old age was a curious thing, she reflected; your bladder worked overtime while your bowels often went on strikes. She had woken up around midnight to use the bathroom and had been awake ever since.

The tin box was still by her bedside. She had forgotten to instruct Tai to put it away. She opened it and, from the bottom, pulled out a large manila envelope secured with an elastic band. Madhura sifted through the letters, photographs and a few yellowing cards. She had even saved Pipi's wedding announcement. The discoloured card bore an embossed peacock. It stated: *Girish and Durga Kanodia seek your blessings on the auspicious occasion of their son Padmakant's wedding to Malti, daughter of Batuk and Jaya Shah, on the 17th of June.*

She couldn't recall if she had cried when she had seen the card. She must have, though not in front of her father. She knew Pipi's parents had been looking for a match for him.

'Girls from good families, fair and homely,' Pipi would tell her, were part of their criteria. 'I heard them talking. And as dowry they will not accept anything less than a Fiat car from the bride's family. Do you have a Fiat-shiat to give them? For you, I will persuade them to even accept a scooter,' he had teased her.

They had already decided he would tell his parents about Madhura when she finished her bachelor's degree. Though he was from an old landholding family, and her father, a salaried employee, was strictly middle class, Pipi insisted that his parents would not be difficult to persuade.

A few months before her final exam, Madhura's father had a stroke. His left hand curled into a grasping claw, his mouth slanted to one side.

They met at Hanging Gardens. Pipi chose a bench facing a giant cement shoe with doors, windows and a sloping roof on top. Children played hide-and-seek, weaving in and out of the playhouse. Pipi repeatedly wiped his face with the white handkerchief he always carried. In between, he took large gulps of the Gold Spot he had brought for the two of them to share.

'There is no one else to look after him, Pipi, and he is bedridden. I can't bring him to your house, can I? My father, instead of a Fiat?' Her mother had passed away when she was a toddler, and it had been just the two of them since then. She couldn't abandon him and move to Surat.

Neither of them questioned tradition. Madhura would look back at this moment and wonder why it was always the girl who had to leave her home and move in with her in-laws. Even if it had occurred to her then to ask Pipi to reverse the norms and come and live with her, it would have been a futile attempt. In the fifties, and even now, it was rare to find a man who would willingly move in with his in-laws.

Back then, she believed Pipi's protests had been half-hearted. His suggestions to wait and see if her father's condition improved, to have faith in God, in destiny, all perfunctory declarations. Years later, he would tell her how he had sobbed on the train back to Surat till an elderly man had offered him a thepla and enquired if someone close to him had passed away.

On the rickety bench across the giant shoe, Madhura saw no signs of the grief that he would later profess at their separation. Eventually, they both fell into silence. Pipi leaned his head against the bench and pointed towards the sky. She followed his gaze, observing vultures gliding towards Hanging Gardens from the Parsi cremation grounds where the dead were laid out to be desiccated by the sun and scavenged by carrion fowl. Then Pipi kissed her on the forehead, tucked his handkerchief into his pocket and walked away. It was all done in one smooth movement, like he had choreographed it in his mind.

She watched him walking downhill through the narrow-paved paths of the terraced garden. He reached the bottom, crossed the street and disappeared into a crowded underpass.

Madhura didn't move from the bench dotted with betel-leaf stains and bird droppings. She continued watching the vultures as she rolled the empty Gold Spot bottle between her palms.

Mornings used to be her favourite time of the day and now they were the most difficult. Before taking her medicines, even getting out of the chair took effort. Arms refusing to push. Feet just flopping on the ground. They had started to scissor, her legs, and it felt like she would have to put a wedge between them when she slept so they didn't cross further.

Raju had called the previous evening, asking if he could bring a colleague along during their lunch break. She didn't feel up to having guests and at first tried making an excuse. He said that they were working at a studio close to her building, and it would just be a short visit.

He arrived soon after lunch with a young girl in tow and asked, 'Madhura Aunty, do you recognize her?'

Madhura could not place the girl with cropped hair and a pierced nose till she heard her speak. A voice like a lychee stripped of its firm peel, a wobbly, liquid sound.

'Miss Desai, you taught me chemistry and were also our dorm matron, Clifton House. Remember?' Anuja said.

She recalled giving Anuja a strict warning after finding all the cards addressed to her on Valentine's Day. The girl had been popular. There had been over a dozen missives of undying love by twelve- and thirteen-year-olds hidden under her mattress.

'She is in charge of all the stills and behind-the-scenes footage for our film,' Raju added.

Anuja, her eyebrows raised, replied in an ironic tone, 'The things I do to pay my credit card bills. But at least I have a credit card, unlike our Raju who is constantly standing in some ATM queue.'

Raju shrugged, 'I prefer cash in my pocket. Some things are better the old-fashioned way, right Madhura Aunty?'

'Well, I prefer making online transactions,' Madhura said.

'Madhura Aunty, you use net banking? At your age?'

'Raju, don't underestimate Miss Desai. During my boarding school days, she set up a computer training room for the neighbouring village. She wasn't just my teacher; her classroom stretched across all of Panchgani. Miss Desai, you had this method of testing where students would move up a seat if they got the right answer. I have still not forgotten the day I moved all the way to the front row.' Anuja clasped Madhura's hand again and said, 'It's so nice to reconnect with you, Miss Desai. I was also wondering if making a small documentary about your case would be all right? I think you have a very interesting story with this plea.'

Madhura's petition had continued making the rounds. It was partly due to the other case where a young man had spent two decades in a vegetative state after being bludgeoned. In the television debates around the legislation regarding euthanasia, Madhura's plea was repeatedly brought up.

Mrs Bharucha had shown her another clip. This one had a religious leader stating that euthanasia

85

could be considered tampering with the cycle of death and reincarnation. The karma of the person seeking euthanasia and the one assisting in the procedure would both be damaged.

It was part of the reason she had finally capitulated and agreed to Mrs Bharucha's television interviews. She was tired of the subjective attributes being tacked on to her plea.

'Anuja, I am already doing a few interviews and I think that should be enough,' she said, elaborating on her meeting with Mrs Bharucha.

'It's an excellent idea to do these interviews,' Anuja said. 'It would add a lot of amazing footage for the documentary too.' She paused and added, 'That is, if you agree to do it. I would just be tagging along with my camera. It would not require any additional effort on your part. The documentary can only lead to a deeper understanding of the subject. And that social worker is right – the government is not going to bother with your plea if you don't drag their attention to it. Every little bit will add up. This is your one big chance, and we should go all guns blazing.'

Anuja then smiled. 'I am glad you are nodding, Miss Desai. Trust me, it will really work out well.'

Getting old was a tragicomedy, Madhura noted. What would Anuja say if she told her that the nodding had nothing to do with acquiescence but were mere tremors. She looked at the young girl who was, in fact, genuinely nodding in agreement. What difference would it make if the girl came with her to the interviews? It seemed churlish to refuse such a small ask.

'Perhaps it is my only chance,' Madhura said, 'or I could literally go – what is the term you used – yes, guns blazing, and murder someone. Then they would have to hang me, wouldn't they?'

When Anuja looked at her in bewilderment, she laughed. 'It's just a joke. And anyway, it wouldn't work. The courts could take pity on me because of my advanced age and, God forbid, give me a life sentence instead.'

The sparrows had disappeared from Bombay. They had been replaced by crows, pigeons and clunkier flying objects. Planes. Specks of metal cut across the grey sky as they drove towards Juhu Beach.

The high tide was swallowing the shore by the time they reached their destination. Raju had planned the entire trip and had also rented the wheelchair kept folded in the trunk. Her own preparations had been restricted to putting on an adult diaper. Experience had taught her that her bladder liked playing practical jokes on her, especially during drives on Bombay's bumpy roads. It had been decided that Raju would take her as far as the concrete embankment and the first line of ice cream stalls.

He parked the wheelchair and hunched beside her on the bench next to the stall selling sugarcane juice. A young boy directed the fibrous cane back and forth through the machine. He then placed two glasses of the frothy juice in their hands.

Madhura was watching a lean man in green shorts. He held a wriggling sea snake in one hand. The man waded in till the waves covered his waist and lowered the creature into the sea. He gently pushed water towards it, his hand creating a tiny flutter, propelling the snake on its way.

'See,' she said, 'a creature struggling in one medium is free in another.'

Raju shook his head, 'I know what you are trying

to say, but I hope they reject your plea.' He wiped the foam moustache off his upper lip as he added, 'You just stay happy, Madhura Aunty, and forget all this.'

He had tried having a similar discussion a few weeks ago. At that point, she had merely changed the topic. But if he was unwilling to let it go, then it would be better to explain her point of view, even if all she wanted to do was enjoy the sunset.

'It's not about being happy or unhappy. I am being practical. What is ahead for me? A major stroke? One that will leave me paralysed? Another fall that I won't completely recover from? When you ask people my age how they want to die, they all say they would like to go in their sleep, but how many get that chance? We all wait till we get cancer and heart attacks. I don't want to do that.' She could not tell him the role his grandfather's illness had played in her decision.

Looking at Raju's despondent face, she tried to lighten the atmosphere. 'To tell you the truth, I have always hated long goodbyes. You won't remember, but even when you people would take the train back, I would tease Pipi that his farewells sometimes lasted longer than the visits. I have always followed the quick band-aid philosophy. Peel it slowly and you keep thinking, "Now it is going to hurt. Oh, it hurts more. Oof, it's really hurting." Better to give it a good yank and pull it off in one go.'

After she was gone, she didn't want this boy to keep asking himself if he had done enough. She knew what it was like to live with that guilt. She tried again, 'Kafka once said, "The meaning of life is that it stops." Think about it, Raju, what if you were watching a movie and it just kept going on without an end. Won't it be meaningless?'

Madhura was unsure if he was serious or merely trying to make her laugh, because, after nodding in agreement, he added, 'I don't know who this Kafka is, but he really sounds like a big bore.'

He then set off to get roasted corn from an adjacent cart – extra chilli and lime for him, less salt for her. Madhura slumped against the backrest of her wheelchair as she watched the sun disappear over the horizon, leaving a pink and violet sky in its trail.

The interviews organized by Mrs Bharucha catapulted Madhura further into the national spotlight. Anuja was exhilarated with the amount of coverage garnered by her former teacher.

'Isn't it so exciting, Miss Desai,' she would say repeatedly, 'you must maintain that balance. Talk about serious matters, and then throw in some of your characteristic one-liners.'

That morning, she had picked Madhura up in her blue Tata Nano. She wanted to take her to Anand Bhavan all the way in Matunga. They wedged her walker into the back and, skirting along the line of discomfort and pain, Madhura folded her limbs into the small car.

'I still get carsick, Miss Desai, but not when I am driving and never like the way I used to on the bus going round and round the Western Ghats till we finally reached school. Vandana and I would both throw up all along the way. You remember Vandana Mathur? She shared a bunk bed with me in Clifton?' Turning towards Madhura, she added, 'You once gave her detention because she stole someone's snacks from the locker, do you know whom I am talking about?'

'Yes, I do. Vandana was a bright girl. She just didn't like the school food, and who could blame her!'

'Miss Desai, you have an amazing memory. I totally get it that you would not forget a student like Freddie Mercury or someone else who became that famous, but you seem to remember all of us.'

When Mrs Bharucha had claimed a connection to Freddie Mercury through her uncle, Madhura had not discussed her own. Farrokh Bulsara, the boy with protruding teeth who insisted on being called Freddie, had been her student when she taught at St Peter's in the early sixties. He had a band even then, she recalled clearly, though the name escaped her – Hermits or Hectics, something like that.

Freddie had struggled with memorizing the periodic table till the day she turned it into a nonsensical verse. She still remembered his voice warbling through, 'hydrogen, helium, lithium, damn, are bigger fools than a BBC (beryllium, boron, carbon) fan.' He had composed a tune on the piano to go with it. The entire class had put on a performance of 'The Element Song', as it was called, at one of the Monday assemblies.

She had always believed that she had been at her happiest when she was with Pipi, but, looking back, Madhura realized that perhaps nothing had given her as much joy as teaching.

Anuja stopped the car outside an eatery with scooters and bicycles crowding the entrance. 'This will translate well on film. We need some variety, otherwise all the indoor shots will look monotonous.'

When their order arrived, she moved the neer dosa and a tumbler of filter coffee closer to Madhura and arranged the bowls of sambar and green chutney on the table. 'We will use these as props right now, but I will order a fresh cup after we finish. It's the best filter coffee in the world!'

When Anuja was satisfied with the arrangements, she said, 'Come, let's try this with you looking right into the lens. Our story would have never been picked up as much if you didn't give them all these great quotes, and you say it with such a poker face too.'

Madhura answered a series of questions before she could finally sip on the promised hot coffee. Anuja wanted her to elaborate further about her hospital stint after the fall.

'Of course, it is connected, Miss Desai. After all, it was shortly after you returned that you sent out your plea?'

She had been placed in a large ward. A curtain away from a man with liver spots on his gleaming scalp, a tube inserted into his windpipe. He used a whiteboard and a black marker to communicate. Two, three words at a time. 'Want Pepsi', 'Take out pipe' and 'Let me go'. Like her, he had no visitors.

The irony of life – she had been completely alone after Pipi's rapid decline, and it was her fall, or rather her decision aided by the fall, that had made people seek her out.

Madhura raised the steel tumbler to her mouth, 'There is nothing to say. I broke a few bones and now I need a walker. Life was anyway limping along earlier, now I am limping with it.'

'That's a good line,' Anuja said. 'Wait, let me write it down so I don't forget. I can do some shots of you walking and then use this as just your voiceover.'

$\sim$

It was early October when the letter arrived. She sat at the dining table, sipping her tea, rereading the letter from the chief justice's office. They had taken over four months to write back to her. A rejection. Carefully worded. Numbers added. NGOs and old people's homes. Typed by one hand and signed by the other, a definitive end to a long wait.

That evening, Madhura made a few additions to her daily to-do list.

1. Have 2 prunes with hot water after dinner
2. Tell Tai to buy washing powder
3. Descale kettle
4. The dhobi has not returned my blue sari. Remember to ask him
5. Pay mobile bill
6. Call Dr Seth. Tell him insomnia is worse. Ask for a prescription. Sleeping pills? Or sleeping pills and antidepressants?
7. Who will go to fill out the prescription?
8. Work out quantity required. 30 pills? Increase by 50% just to be on the safe side as 20% of all medicines are apparently counterfeit.
9. Amass adequate quantity
10. Would a note be required to ensure that Tai and Raju are not harassed by the police for aiding and abetting suicide?
11. Fix a date based on procurement plan

Preceded by three short bursts of the doorbell, Tikku, the little girl next door, would amble in with her backpack. Even though Madhura usually played old Hindi songs or her Queen albums from three to four-thirty in the afternoon, she would switch off the music on Tikku's arrival.

Like Mrs Bharucha, Tikku had also been ushered into the house by Tai. She had found the girl sitting on the staircase and had brought her into the flat.

Tikku's first day in the Desai household had been a noteworthy one. A loquacious girl with a heart-shaped face and a shadowy moustache, she asked questions incessantly and, fortunately, answered most herself.

'You don't go to the office? My Daddy also doesn't go and, like you, he also works on the computer. Do you play games on the computer? I also play. Whom do you play with?'

'The computer,' Madhura replied without looking away from her screen. Her feet were swollen like two inflatable rafts, and she was feeling irritable.

'But you can play with other people also. I play ludo on Daddy's laptop. I have asked him to make an account for me, but he doesn't have time. You play ludo?'

'Yes, but I haven't played in a long time.'

'It's easy. Come, I will show you. We can be partners.'

'No,' Madhura said, 'I prefer playing chess.'

'Let's play ludo! You will see, it's too much fun.'

Madhura reluctantly made an account and the game began – Madhura and Tikku against an unknown player. After he killed their green pawn, he sent a message, 'Hi!'

Madhura ignored it, but Tikku typed back, 'Hi!'

Then came the next message. 'Show me your boobs.'

Fumbling while attempting to switch the computer off, Madhura finally threw a towel over the monitor as Tikku watched in bewilderment.

It was past seven that evening when Tikku's mother stood on the doorstep looking for her daughter. Madhura had seen the young woman rushing across the common corridor. She would run down the stairs early in the morning holding her daughter's hand. Evenings, she usually trudged up alone with files or vegetable-laden plastic bags like the one she was currently holding.

'The lady on the third floor said she saw Tikku coming to your place. She is not supposed to leave the flat like this.'

Tikku, with a leaking nose and eyes about to follow suit, said, 'I rang the doorbell and knocked. Daddy didn't open the door. Mama, don't get upset. Next time I will wait on the steps for you.'

Madhura watched the woman embrace her daughter. She noticed the hollows under her eyes, the glass bangles gliding over old scars on her left wrist when she stretched her arms across her daughter's back.

'Tai also knocked next door, but no one answered,' Madhura said. 'I am home all the time. In case there is a problem again, Tikku can always wait here for you. She is welcome to come here whenever she likes.'

~

Late into the night, Madhura had started spreading the contents of the manila envelope across her bed. She had stored all their letters, including the ones she had written to Pipi over the years. Unable to post them to Surat, she used to hand them over to him during his visits.

His lips would move as he read, silently forming the words. He would then lick his finger and flick over to the next sheet. After he finished, he would fold the letters into whimsical shapes – ducks, rabbits and once even a cow. Since he had to use rectangular sheets of paper instead of squares, these creatures would sport extra wings and sometimes one leg. He would then prop them up on her dining table. She knew he could not take the letters home.

After Pipi got married, there was a period of twenty-odd years when they didn't see each other. She met him again at her aunt Kusum's funeral, a sombre occasion shadowed by the aftermath of the Emergency and Indira Gandhi's recent electoral defeat. Her father would have been devastated. Nehru had been his idol. Her father had bought their first radio when a neighbour had told him that Nehru's speech as the first prime minister of India would be broadcast live close to midnight on the 14th of August.

Funny tricks her mind played these days. It wandered like a dog let off the leash, sniffing out and chewing on whatever it found – desiccated corn cobs and dead birds, Nehru, Pipi, her father, Indira.

Like her, Pipi had come to offer condolences. They were both in their forties by then. There was a softness to the edge of his chin, the line of his shoulders. He looked prosperous and content as he stood amidst a group of men, all in white kurtas. He looked in her direction, distantly at first, and then his eyes steadied as he recognized her.

It was a hushed conversation, Pipi keeping his voice down like the others in the room. Questions. The kind you ask acquaintances. About jobs and relatives. Then he asked if she still lived on Tilak Road. She told him that after her father had passed away, she had taken a teaching job at a boarding school in Panchgani. She would be in Bombay for the summer break and then would return to Panchgani. He said work brought him to Bombay often and asked if he could come and have tea with her the following Tuesday.

He arrived two hours late, with the air of conviviality that he always carried with him. The train had been delayed, he said, offering her a newspaper-wrapped package as an apology. It was the first time he brought her vada pav from the station, a tradition that would last for over four decades. Madhura never told him that she didn't like pav.

She had just a few pictures of them together. People usually took photographs on their holidays, but they had never been on one. It had largely been the two of them spending time at her flat and occasionally going for long drives and to the racecourse. Perhaps she wasn't as comfortable as Pipi about lying to people about their relationship, or she had simply been content, but, over the years, Madhura slowly cut herself off from neighbours and friends. Her life had revolved around her students and classes and, during the holidays, Pipi. When she retired from teaching, it had been only Pipi.

Her fingers were twitching again, as if she were trying to fan herself with the Polaroid she had picked up from the bed. It had been taken on her fiftieth birthday. Her hair was in a bun, with a rose tucked incongruously behind her ear. Pipi, with his characteristic smile that didn't curve at the ends but lit up his face in a horizontal line, sat opposite her, his grey hair pushed away from his broad forehead.

Even by Pipi's standards, it was an extravagant

meal at Sea Rock Hotel's revolving restaurant. The restaurant rotated on a conveyor belt, a carousel where tables and chairs laden with Chinese dishes replaced rocking horses. They timed it – Pipi and her – the restaurant took exactly thirty-six minutes to complete a circuit.

Madhura was used to roadside eateries where food was placed on large steel plates and napkins were a rarity. She only ordered one dish – vegetable spring rolls – partly because the rotating motion of the restaurant made her stomach feel queasy and also because of the extravagant prices printed on the menu. She felt out of place in her plain sari and Kolhapuri sandals sitting beside the wealthy and the famous in their printed chiffons. When she told Pipi this, he plucked a rose from the bud vase on their table. He broke the stem and tucked the flower into her hair. He told her she looked like the famous Doordarshan newsreader Salma Sultan.

Among the waiters carrying platters of Chicken Manchurian and American Chop Suey, a photographer with a Polaroid camera stopped at tables and offered to take pictures of the guests. Pipi called out to him. 'Take a nice picture-shicture of us,' he said, and then, in a louder voice, as if he thought he owed the man an explanation, as well as anyone else watching them, he added, 'It's my cousin's birthday.'

He told her that the first revolving restaurant was not this one in Bombay, as the newspapers claimed, but in his Surat. 'However, the food is better here,' he added.

Madhura wondered if he had gone there with his wife. If he had tucked roses into her hair too. In the beginning, there had been guilt and even a sense of shame about his marital status. She didn't know if it had disappeared over time or she had just blocked it out.

She once asked Pipi if anyone questioned him about their relationship. He hesitated at first and then said, 'My son brought it up. Now don't feel bad, but I had to say these things, I just told him that Madhura Ben is related to us and she is all by herself. I go to meet her because I feel bad for her.'

Though she knew Pipi would deny it, she felt that his decision to sometimes bring Raju to Bombay was more than about exposing him to a wider world beyond Surat as he claimed. It was also calculated to deflect any suspicions his family, especially his wife, Malti, may have had.

Pipi rarely mentioned his wife or spoke about his life in Surat. In a way, living in two different cities made it easier, not just for Pipi, but for her as well. She could pretend that when he left her flat, he simply disappeared into the ether.

Sea Rock Hotel was gone. It never recovered from the terrorist blasts of 1993. It stood there, an empty shell, shattered glass panes facing the sea, the facade crumbling away until it was razed to the ground two decades later.

⁓

A round of bingo was the order of the day at Tikku's suggestion. Raju had been elected the announcer and he pulled out a token from the red bag and declared, 'Three and three, ice cream is free.'

Thirty-three seemed to be a popular number because there were responding squeals, especially from Tai sitting in the far corner. Her two-hour cleaning stint was over, but she had decided to stay back to play the game. The coffee table was covered with plates of samosas brought over by Tikku's mother. Madhura had found it difficult to mark the numbers on her scorecard and Tikku had taken over the task for her. The game of bingo ended when Raju announced, 'Eight and eight, two uncles on a date,' and Tai, screeching in excitement, almost fell off the stool when she won the Housie.

At first, having people in her flat had irked Madhura. The noise, scuffed footprints on the floor, a glass toppled over by a careless hand. It had taken her time to get used to the idea of people dropping by and meals that consisted of more than curd rice or plain roti with dal.

After the game, there was still time to do some division sums with Tikku. Madhura played a maths game with her, using an egg carton and the deshelled peas heaped on the table. In the last few weeks, Tikku's mother had repeatedly proposed a small compensation for the tutoring, but Madhura had declined the offer.

When they finished the lessons, Tikku showed her a pamphlet on butterflies she had brought from the library. 'They are so amazing! First, they are caterpillars and then they change. You know what else is amazing? Poop! It has the same spelling back and front.'

Madhura admonished her for using an unrefined word, but the girl had a way of putting things that made her smile.

In her younger days, when people asked her if she regretted not having children, she had usually answered in monosyllables to get them off the topic. It had rarely bothered her. Her life had been filled with the cacophony of young and energetic minds. As a dorm matron, her small room, with its own bathroom, a hot plate and a flimsy door, had been located within a large hall with almost fifty young girls.

When she would come home for the holidays, the solitude of her flat would feel like a sanctuary. She could not pinpoint the day when the silence in her home with its leaky ceiling had started feeling overwhelming or when she had started playing music to fill the afternoon stillness.

After Tikku left, Madhura opened her bedside cabinet to check if she had any digestive pills. Her stomach was not used to deep-fried samosas any more. The sleeping pills she had collected lay in the drawer. She picked them up. The strips glistening within her trembling fingers as they caught the light at differing angles.

Madhura sat by the window and watched the dogs again. She liked observing them. They lived in different tenses, the dogs and her, they bounded around in the only one they knew – the present – while she meandered in the past.

The bingo game had brought back memories of her days in Panchgani. It wasn't just the school, but she had also been involved with the local farmers. She would organize bingo games every Sunday as an incentive to get them to join her computer classes. When their strawberry plantations had started failing in the seventies, she had been part of a group of locals that had tried to find ways to boost the yield. Madhura had vivid memories of the days spent with a straw hat on her head, digging into the soil, inhaling the smell of wet earth and sweat, as they tried different methods to increase the production. She had a separate toothbrush to scrub the dirt out of her nails. A few times in the dark, she had grabbed it accidentally, tasting the gritty soil mixed with minty toothpaste.

Pipi had come to meet her once during that period. He had stayed in the small Parsi hotel uphill from the school. Madhura didn't know what he had said at home. She had not asked. After that trip, she had written to him:

The closest I can come to describing what it's like being with you is that it feels like I am sucking on a boiled sweet. Tucking it into a cheek so that it will last longer but I have to constantly resist the urge to bite into it.

Ironically, their relationship had lasted till his wife passed away three years ago. Pipi's condition deteriorated rapidly after Malti's death. He lost weight, became wan. When he would call her from his office, he would keep muttering about how he had wronged her for so many years, how he had been unfair to her. 'That's why God took her from me, I didn't deserve her,' he would say during their phone calls.

It was the only time in their long relationship that she realized Pipi and his wife had shared a close bond. Malti had rarely occupied her thoughts when she was alive. Madhura had relegated her to the back of her mind like unappealing Diwali gifts shoved in overhead cabinets. When he used to describe his days in Surat, or how he liked sitting in his garden, the one he said was filled with so many fruit trees that it was like an orchard, she had always imagined him alone.

Raju had recently told her that his grandparents liked playing carom together in the garden. 'They would place little bets on the game. If they saw me passing by, I would be forced to play with them too.'

It had been easy to discount their life together since she had never witnessed them playing these games, sharing their morning tea, discussing their children, all the customary practices of a married couple.

On Pipi's last visit to Bombay, he insisted he had to go to see Genius. His hands were fluttering around his neck in circular motions like he was wrapping a gift. She finally realized that he was tying an invisible tie. He always wore a tie to the racecourse.

'Genius is dead, Pipi,' she tried telling him.

'What a joke! I just saw him yesterday.'

'No, he passed away years ago.'

He frowned at her. 'You are lying.'

'No, why would I?'

Pipi gazed at her, his head tilting to one side. 'I don't like this silly game-wame. Stop it now.'

He picked up an orange from the fruit basket on her dining table. By the time he had finished peeling the orange, he had forgotten about Genius. He asked her to put on his favourite ghazals. He seemed to remember the lyrics and hummed along easily. Then he told her he had to go meet his mother. She had promised to buy him a car and he didn't want to upset her by being late. There was no point in reminding him that his mother had passed away decades ago.

Madhura didn't know how he had managed the journey to Bombay, but she could not send him back alone. She booked two train tickets to Surat and took him home.

The morning light filtered in through the window grille and embroidered her arm with its shifting patterns. Madhura drew the curtains further back to look at the sun illuminating the buildings across the street. Despite the water damage and a few boarded-up windows, the buildings had a festive air about them with their washing lines in the balconies filled with boxers and bright saris like buntings strung across a party hall.

It was a quarter past ten and according to her schedule, it was time for her to read the paper. These days, even with her glasses, she struggled to read the smaller fonts. She would have to get her eyes retested she decided, as the letters blurred together below the headlines. Placing the paper further away helped, and she was halfway through, when her morning was disrupted by Mrs Bharucha's arrival.

In the weeks after her plea was rejected by the government, Mrs Bharucha, after an initial burst of bristling emails to various ministers and writing an open letter in the Sunday edition of the *Times of India*, had been conspicuously absent.

Settling into one of Madhura's rickety chairs and without wasting a moment in exchanging pleasantries, she began, 'I know how disappointed you have been. No, let me correct that, how disappointed *we* have all been. But where there is a will, there is a way or, rather, I will always find a way.'

She said that she had written to Dignitas, a non-profit-assisted dying organization in Switzerland. There was a membership to be obtained with an annual fee. Similar to joining any local club, except, instead of offering you squash lessons or a beer by the poolside, you could avail yourself of a swift death with a small dose of a lethal drug.

'There are numerous procedures to be followed and I didn't want to tell you before it was finalized. First, we had to send them information about your plea and medical records. But they have agreed to take you on! Isn't that good news?'

'Yes,' Madhura said, her voice sounding strange to her own ears.

'Just a few more formalities, we have to get some evaluations that certify you are not depressed and are capable of making independent decisions, and then you can be on your way to Zurich,' Mrs Bharucha added. 'You know, there are so many people following this story for whom you are a symbol of hope. Just last week, I received a letter from a man with ALS. He said he read about you and realized that if a woman can take such a brave and bold step, then why as a man is he fearing the inevitable. A bit misogynistic – this man stronger than woman business – if you ask me, but that's not the point.'

Mrs Bharucha continued the conversation in her usual unflappable manner, as if she was dictating the recipe for making roast chicken. Slicing, dicing, making stock from giblets.

'And, don't worry, I will start an online fundraiser

so that we can send you in style, no economy, only business class for our icon. Isn't this wonderful news?'

Madhura looked down at the table. 'This is so . . .' she said, her mouth opening and closing repeatedly, forming sentences and dismissing them, before settling on, 'unexpected. I am not sure how to . . .'

Mrs Bharucha interrupted her, 'You don't have to thank me. This is what I do, help people in need. On the way to our office, I remember you telling me, "I want to walk across the finishing line instead of waiting to suffer and then have to be dragged across it." It moved me deeply, your courage. And now it's finally happening!'

'Ten Green Bottles' of the childhood ditty flashed in her mind. Words, behaving like they were made of glass, falling back into her throat, one by one, till there were none left.

~

'I get to feelin', I was back in the old days, long ago, when we were kids, when we were young,' Freddie's voice warbled out of the speaker as she sat in front of her computer with a scratch pad and a pen.

Reasons to go, she wrote on the left side of the paper. *Reasons to stay*, on the right. Sometimes she was convinced that seeking death on her own terms was the only way ahead, then, a moment later, the fear returned.

She jotted down six logical reasons, one below the other, on the left side of the paper. The right side below the header remained blank. At least if she believed in God, she could have imagined a heaven somewhere. Krishna, Jesus, it didn't matter which god or whose god as long as she wasn't alone. She didn't even have that small comfort. Instead, the image that came repeatedly to her mind was of the earthworms readied for dissection in the science lab. Stranded on the sterile station, wriggling away as the students armed with dissecting pins and hand lens loomed over them.

She sat staring at the blank column till the album ended. *Innuendo* had released a few months before Freddie passed away. They had named an asteroid after him last year on what would have been his seventieth birthday. She wondered if he had felt this overwhelming panic close to the end or had gone like the shooting star he had likened himself to in one of his songs.

～

'Gita, shift the light to the left,' Anuja instructed her assistant as Madhura waited for them to set up. On being introduced, Gita bent towards Madhura and gave her a hug, unexpected and exuberant.

'I read all about you,' she said. 'You have inspired me to donate my organs. Like you always say, every part of our body should be utilized and this way I will leave something behind too.'

Madhura felt trapped on the couch, like an insect pinned to the mounting board, hoping the girl would move away. Fortunately, Anuja interrupted the conversation. 'You know, Gita, that gorgeous lotus tattoo you have on your calf? Along with your eyes and kidneys, donate that bit of skin also. It can be turned into a nice coin purse for your mom. Each time she pays the milkman, she will pull out her little bag and feel comforted knowing she always has a part of you with her.'

Anuja's sarcasm was not appreciated by Gita, who, ignoring the comment, began rummaging through the equipment box.

When they were ready, Madhura was asked to sit on the rattan chair by the window. Adjusting the starched sari with her unsteady hands, she looked directly at the camera and repeated her line, 'It is death that gives significance to our lives.'

'Let's try saying this more naturally, Miss Desai. This feels like you have memorized it.'

Year after year, Madhura would dissuade her students from rote learning by scribbling across dusty blackboards, 'Parrots only look good flying across the sky and not in my classroom.'

Now she had turned into one. Regurgitating meaningless sentences. She turned away, lowering her spectacles, rubbing her eyes as if weariness could be wiped clean.

'Keep looking out of the window,' Anuja said. 'The sun is creating a nice, striated effect.'

Holding her position for the camera, Madhura watched the autorickshaws, black and yellow with rounded hoods, scurrying over potholed roads. A swarm of bumblebees whizzing between dented buses. While Pipi had favoured the insulation of cars with their rolled-up windows, Madhura had always looked for excuses to hail a rickshaw. Journeys that began with the clanking sound of the metre being pushed down. Congested streets turning into her own radio station, with a playlist of impatient horns. Even the stench of drying fish on the Khar–Danda Road had not dissuaded her from her preferred mode of transport. Metre down, moving along, speeding up, slowing down. Till it had all come to a standstill. Parked in one place, the metre still ticking away.

'Are you feeling all right, Miss Desai? Do you want a quick coffee break?' Anuja asked as Madhura continued staring out of the window.

'I am a bit tired,' she replied.

'Of course! Gita, will you go down to Starbucks and get Miss Desai a latte and a black coffee for me, please?'

Coffee at this hour meant a sleepless night. Another one. Sitting in her chair, letting the darkness seep into her skin, crawl in through her eyes.

When the bell rang, it was not the assistant but Raju, who had returned from the market. Madhura could see his bushy eyebrows lift, the shine in his eyes unconcealed by their frequent blinking. He had a crush, she suspected, and one that would go unrequited. Overhearing Anuja on the phone, Madhura had gathered she had a boyfriend.

A headphone with superior acoustics, Madhura's bathroom sucked in sound through its ventilation duct. Brushing her teeth, she would hear screaming children and quarrelling couples as they traversed the common corridor. A few days ago, her name drifted in through the duct.

'Yes, Miss Desai is finally going to Switzerland. Isn't that amazing? I mean, I love the old lady, but this will be the perfect end for the film. Shit! Do you think that I am a bad person? To think like this?' A short burst of laughter and Anuja continued, 'Max and I will come to see you after this trip. Shut up! What kind of a friend are you? Of course, I'm still with him, it's serious between us.'

Though it had been a jolt to realize that her death was such a highly anticipated event, she didn't blame Anuja. The girl was merely partaking of what had been on offer.

'Anuja,' Raju asked, 'hope you are staying for dinner?'

'I can't, Mrs Bharucha is expecting me. We have to finish making all the arrangements for the big party,' she replied with a wide grin. 'Have you decided what you will wear, Miss Desai? I thought you could do that lilac sari?'

'I have given the sari to Tai.'

'Oh, that's sweet. Doesn't matter, we will find something else.'

Madhura made another attempt. 'Let's not have the party. It's too much of a fuss.'

'But you were happy with the idea, and it's all been organized now,' Anuja said with a forced brightness like she was cajoling a toddler. 'I was not going to tell you, but Raju said you love Jackie Shroff and we have managed to get him to attend!'

Madhura turned towards Raju in puzzlement. 'He was working on our set last week. You saw him in *Rangeela* and liked him,' Raju added. 'I had put it on, remember?'

'Jackie is coming to meet you, Miss Desai. You can't back out now,' Anuja said.

Back out of the party. She didn't know if she wanted to back out all the way. In the last few days, she had tried finding the certainty she had had during the initial interviews Mrs Bharucha had set up. But the conviction with which she had written her plea and spoken to journalists was missing.

She tried reminding herself of Seung Sahn's teachings where he stated that at different temperatures, water may change to ice or steam but it did not disappear. Name and form may alter, but the composition, H_2O, like your true self, stays the same. But the comfort she had found in the Zen master's ideology had dissipated.

Sometimes she thought she had been undermined by greed as much as fear. A craving for another helping on a full stomach. Teaching Tikku, sharing her curry recipe with Tai, hearing Raju's flat-footed shuffle in the living room had revived her neglected appetite for life. 'Little more,' her heart, with its own cluster of forty thousand neurons howled, subjugating her rational mind.

Madhura decided that she would put up with the party and then leave Bombay. That night, ignoring the clamouring of her knotted leg, Madhura tried dragging the suitcase out from under her bed and failed. She would have to ask Tai to get it out for her. She considered what she would need to pack.

The envelope with her pictures and letters, eight of her favourite saris, her mother's supari box. She pictured the small suitcase stuffed with her precious belongings. Like she was a twenty-year-old, about to elope with an unsuitable man.

Anuja would be disappointed and Mrs Bharucha livid. Her world of campaigns, interviews, forming human chains, brandishing misspelt but politically correct placards was a narrow enclosure. There was no space for turning around.

The logistics would have to be planned. And she would need help. With her bag. Down to the gate and into an autorickshaw. 'Santacruz Station,' she would tell the driver; from there, it didn't matter, Karjat or Jalgaon, as long as no one could find her, ask her questions. Jitu, she considered, she could ask him to come up for her bag.

⁓

Mrs Bharucha's ostentatious living room was crowded, and the samosas were stale. Sitting beside her, Sharda had taken one bite and complained about the quality of the snacks being served. Another component in her breathless litany that started with the dirty train station and a rude taxi driver.

There would be about forty guests, Madhura had been told. Who were these people who had come to her grand farewell, she wondered, and where had they been in the last decade? Was it just human nature to ignore the living and pay homage to the dead, or, in her case, the nearly departed?

She had been placed in a tall carved armchair in front of a cleared-out space meant to function as a makeshift stage. There was a mike in the centre and on one side an easel with a large photograph of Madhura. The sole missing element was a garland of white flowers around her picture that would signify a deceased status. How many people get to attend their own funeral, she noted as Mrs Bharucha ushered a few of her friends towards her. They all had trite clichés to offer. 'You are so brave' seemed to be the catchphrase of the evening.

What would they say when she slipped away? Even Sharda would be bewildered by her actions, or perhaps she would tell her son, 'I knew it, she was always a big fraud.' Only Pipi, slumped in a flanking chair, would not judge her.

Raju had persuaded his mother to bring Pipi along as a surprise. With a handkerchief pinned to his kurta using a large safety pin and neatly combed hair, Pipi remained largely silent, occasionally muttering to himself. In the past, she would have teased him if he was cursing under his breath at being dragged to a party without a glass of whiskey to make it tolerable. On this occasion, it would be pointless. Her initial joy at seeing him at Mrs Bharucha's had evaporated when he looked at her with those rheumy, blank eyes without a hint of recognition.

His absence was not a constant ache, nor did it come equipped with a full stop. It lived between pauses and emerged at unexpected moments. There were times she could pretend that he was just away in Surat, and then there were days when, playing chess or drinking tea, she felt the emptiness so acutely that it was difficult to breathe. She grieved for him like he had passed away. At least that would have been some sort of closure. He was alive, her Pipi, but just a shell, like Sea Rock Hotel – unoccupied, crumbling – until he too was razed to the ground.

Sharda, prattling away about Bombay's traffic, stopped mid-sentence, looking over Madhura's shoulder in flushed reverence. Jackie Shroff had arrived. The limited time he had allotted meant that Mrs Bharucha immediately ushered him towards the stage, beaming away in a manner that looked like she was stretching her lips to brush her teeth.

Clearing his throat, the actor looked around the room, a bewildered expression on his face before it was covered with practised ease. 'When I was told that having me here was Madhura ji's last wish, I was deeply humbled,' he began.

Madhura almost shook her head before catching herself. Anuja had hired an extra cameraperson to cover the event and he was constantly three feet away from her face.

'What a story! I would have loved to star in it, if only the audience would accept me as an eighty-year-old woman.' He paused with a smile and raised his palms to signal the tittering audience to settle down. 'But we are not here to talk about movies. This is about Madhura Desai, who is changing the way we think about life and its counterpart – death. Let's have a round of applause for the real star among us!'

Sharda's enthusiastic claps echoed in her ears. A drumming that made the sides of her head pulse in unison. 'How long do we have to stay here?' she asked Raju.

'We need to wait, Madhura Aunty. I still don't agree with what you are doing, but there are many guests here who think it is a great cause and they all want to meet you one last time.'

She stifled the urge to tell Raju her plan when she heard his voice break on the last few words.

Passing the mike was the party game being played at Mrs Bharucha's. After the actor, it was the hostess who held centre stage. Listing the steps she had taken to ensure what she called 'Madhura ji's most fervent desire', she continued her speech with 'Of course we must ensure that legislation is built in so that the law is not misused, but euthanasia is not a sin nor is it, as many may have stated, against Indian culture. Let me remind them of the concept of Prayopavesa, the Hindu practice that advocates suicide by fasting for a person who has no desire and responsibilities remaining in life. It is also allowed in cases of terminal disease or grave disabilities. Savarkar also renounced life and fasted to death. Madhura Desai is not just availing of the right to lawful euthanasia but is paving the way for others.'

Looking at the guests nodding away, Madhura had to concede that Mrs Bharucha had the gift of persuasion. An asset in her line of work. Cajole or bulldoze, she would get her way. This was her attempt at turning Madhura into a symbol, a plus or multiplication sign that could be added to Mrs Bharucha's future equations. She wondered how Mrs Bharucha would spin the story around her disappearance.

There were other speakers, some who worked with Mrs Bharucha and a few suffering from terminal illnesses, like a frail young man with non-Hodgkin lymphoma. Along with members of his support group, he had decided to start a petition to legalize active euthanasia. 'Miss Desai is setting the ground for us to move forward,' he said, 'and haven't people like us suffered enough? Shouldn't we have the option of ending it in a painless manner?'

Her mind felt like a wobble board, moving side to side with shifting weight. Though she had a diaper on, Madhura used the bathroom as an excuse to leave the room and compose herself.

In the dim foyer that led to the powder room, she was stopped by a middle-aged couple who had just arrived.

'Madhura Desai?' the woman asked, as the man with sunken cheeks and a jaundiced tone to his skin watched from his wheelchair. 'Samir, my husband, and I have come from Pune to meet you. He insisted,' she added, patting her husband on the arm, a gesture of gentle affection.

'Madhura ji,' he said, his words slurred, like he had been drinking all evening, an impression negated by the strain on his face as he tried to get the words out. 'You have given us strength.'

Samir Kadam had motor neurone disease, she learned with his wife's help. He had been diagnosed last March and had been told that, along with gradually losing the ability to communicate, he would deteriorate to the point where he would be unable to swallow and, eventually, breathe. There was no cure.

'When he said he would want it to end when he could not do things for himself, I could not bear the idea. Then he showed me your interview. I don't know why, but it calmed me,' she said.

Samir, drawing each word out, added, 'I can't control anything, but, looking at you, I know I can have some control over my death.'

127

'Enough, Sam,' his wife said. Her eyes were damp, Madhura noted. Love and loss, emotions at disparate ends of the thermostat, condensing, the way water vapour deposits itself on cold glass windows.

He smiled. 'Yes, enough. That's what I feel too. All this time, I kept asking myself – is this all? When, Madhura ji, you have given me the courage to say "this is enough".'

Madhura rolled down the window. The sky was devoid of stars, except for one, a solitary pinhole of light hovering below the waxing moon. She was sitting beside Pipi in the rear seat of Raju's car. After muttering for a few minutes in Gujarati, Pipi asked her if Nita had come back. She didn't know anyone called Nita.

Sharda, without turning around from the front, called out, 'Yes, she is here.' Then, in a hushed tone, she said, 'Have to keep reassuring him, Madhura Ben, otherwise he gets agitated. And please wipe his nose. It must be leaking; he has a bad cold,' she added, like Pipi was in another room and not sitting right behind her.

If age had to strip us of all dignity, then it was best it should take away our awareness too, Madhura considered. Pipi was lucky in a way. Spared by the deterioration of his mind. Unlike her father. Lying in bed for years. His left side paralysed. His kurta always had stains despite her best efforts. Pants swapped for lungis. Easier to slip bedpans in and out. It was difficult to admit, but, with time, the respect along with the love she had for her father had faded away within the overwhelming odour of illness and decay. She still carried the guilt of feeling relief instead of grief when he passed away.

At the party, people had called her brave, when her one courageous act had been choosing to stay with her father when he fell ill. But it had slowly eroded her. Altered her into someone who preferred escape instead of acceptance. Taking a job at a boarding school right after her father's death to distract herself from her loneliness. Her unwillingness to think about Pipi's wife. The refusal to check on Pipi's condition after his illness made him immobile. Her plea had also been a bid to escape her failing body. Now, finally, when the death she had asked for was handed to her, she wanted to run away from it too.

The car stopped at a traffic light and, in the darkened rear lit by the occasional headlights of passing cars, Pipi looked at her, patted her hair and said, 'Thank you, Nita.'

She clasped his hand and squeezed it tightly, holding it till they reached her building.

Sharda dropped her to the flat and pushed open the squeaking door for her. On her way to the kitchen, Madhura bumped into the dining table with her walker. It was right here, a few feet from the table, where she had collapsed. Even in excruciating pain she had been aware of the stench from her soiled sari. On the floor, alone, waiting for the end. Well, alone except for the spider staring back at her with its eight eyes.

'Strangers in the night, exchanging glances', the lyrics of a Frank Sinatra song dropped into her head, followed by a bout of laughter at the image of a duet between her and the spider. She immediately felt a dampness. The laughter had put too much pressure on her bladder. Emotional incontinence followed by actual incontinence. At least she still had her diaper on.

The finishing line – one way or another – was right ahead. She had told Mrs Bharucha that walking was better than being dragged across it. Here she had the opportunity to choose a death that had some meaning. And what was the alternative? To wait. Till she wasted away. Like her Pipi.

Eighty-six years. She had seen the British leave India. Watched Mahatma Gandhi speak at Sarojini Naidu's house; no, it was someone else with a similar name – yes, Sumati Morarjee's home. Gone from reading about rockets to seeing the first moon landing. Had loved Pipi deeply and been loved in return. She had even heard the great Freddie Mercury sing, only for her, a private audience of one, with the lyrics she had made up. Like that poor Samir Kadam had said – it was enough.

People called life a gift, but it was a loan. All briefly borrowed. Instead of slamming the door on her creditor, she would go ahead and befriend him. Like she was calling him over for a cup of coffee and saying, 'You don't have to keep lurking around waiting to clobber me when I am not looking. Let's end this on a good note. Here is what I owe you and it's already been slightly overdue.'

Madhura took a glass of water into the bedroom and had her pills. In half an hour, the pain would subside to tolerable levels. She propped open the canvas flap of her suitcase against the wall and began emptying her bag of its meagre treasures. It was a slow process. Picking up things and dropping them repeatedly with her fumbling fingers. The pictures and letters she would tear and throw away. Tai would be pleased with her small gold earrings and her saris. Her mother's supari box. She opened it, looking at the date engraved in the right corner – 1931. A present from her father on the day she was born. Perhaps Tikku could use it to store her little stickers. Something to remember her by.

Madhura left her toilet kit and the few pieces of clothing she would need for Zurich inside the suitcase. Wednesday morning, she would be off. Off. A funny word that one. She had heard people use it, especially in Bombay, to denote death. Off on a journey. Or off like a light switch. She wasn't quite sure what it meant.

Welcome to Paradise

When her mother called, Garima didn't pick up the phone. It was Neil who gave her the news. 'She says it's an emergency. They are going to cut off her power supply.'

Garima took a flight to Goa the next morning, expecting to spend the day talking to municipal officers. She was led to the garden instead.

'You always keep things to yourself,' Leela began, her face streaked with mud as she planted a line of sunflowers, 'but, luckily, Neil had the sense to tell me what has happened.'

She wondered if he had told her mother the same things – he had not meant to cheat. He got carried away with his friends.

'Leave it, Ma. What's the problem with the municipal board?'

Leela held Garima by the arm and led her to a rickety bench. 'First, I want to talk about you. Neil told me you stay awake all night, barely eat. You can't torture yourself like this. Have you tried speaking to someone, a professional?'

She had found a therapist. Her anxiety increasing as she sat on the faux-leather couch in the reception. Garima picked at one end of the couch as she waited, till she could see the orange sponge underneath. One material, pretending to be another and hiding a third. Pulling off her own layers in front of a stranger seemed beyond her capabilities. She left without informing the receptionist.

Her mother continued, 'You know, these things happen.'

She had once seen her mother's smile making things happen as well. It had been at an art gallery. Leela, in a printed sari, her silver earrings swinging with the motion, turned in Garima's direction. It lit up her face – that two-vodkas-down, joyful grin. Garima followed its trajectory, like it was a beam shooting out from her mother's gleaming teeth. She

134

swivelled, looking behind her at a bespectacled man, the recipient, flushing in delight.

'Maybe they do happen, Ma – to you. I don't want to live like that. I stick by my commitments, and I expect the same in return.'

'I agree, but people slip sometimes.'

'Slipping hurts other people. Like Dad. Or, have you forgotten?'

'Garima, there are things about him that I can't discuss, especially not with you. But he wasn't some perfect hero. For that matter, no one is, including Neil.'

'That seems clear. And he didn't even have the guts to tell me himself!'

'What would that achieve aside from hurting you?' her mother asked. 'It's like scarfing down a carton of ice cream which you then throw up on someone else. Leaving them to clean the mess.'

Leela stroked Garima's hair and said, 'I know you are hurt. But you can't go through life without some amount of pain. There is a poem – by Jane Hitchfield or some field; I forget her last name – "So few grains of happiness measured against all the dark and still the scales balance."'

Garima wrestled with an urge to bang her head on the bench. Repeatedly. Till her mother's scraped-together philosophical drone ended. Then the entire family would hear about 'poor Garima and her hysterical behaviour'. Stalling was the only sensible move.

'Let's talk later. I am exhausted.'

Leela nodded. 'These early morning flights are a pain. It was not an emergency, though. I just lied to Neil. But now that you are here, you can sort out a small matter. These municipal officers want to know why the electricity bill is still in Martin Rebello's name. How does it matter? He is dead. Who do they think is paying the bill, his ghost?'

Garima spent the afternoon upending drawers in her mother's house, looking for the misplaced title deed. Leela, who had disappeared into her studio at the far end of the property, emerged hours later in her paint-splattered kaftan, tooting the horn of a scooter.

'A car is a cage. All you can smell is recycled bad breath,' she said, refusing to get into their old Maruti.

Garima asked about helmets. Leela shrugged, the scooter wobbling as she hitched up her kaftan and adjusted her bottom on the sticky seat.

They hurtled over speed breakers on a potholed road with hawkers selling sarongs on one side. The smell of fermenting cashew apple from the nearby alcohol stills filled the air as they reached a narrow lane. When they stopped, Garima swung one leg over, trying to get off, and the bike toppled over. The spill made her grumpy. When her mother asked her if she was hurt, she shook her head in a brisk manner and walked ahead.

'I should have told you, Garu,' Leela called out as she caught up with her, 'don't get off the scooter till I put the stand down first.'

At the end of the lane, there was a shack with a low thatched roof. Sandcastle, it said in faded letters at the entrance. Unfamiliar music streamed out of boxy speakers. Indian music mixed for Western ears. She followed her mother inside.

'Order a lemongrass tea for me,' Leela said before striding towards the bathroom.

Garima was watching a woman dancing in a stupor when she felt a tug on her foot and let out a startled yelp. A dog had curled around her leg and two more had settled down beside her.

A wiry man, bare-chested, like a large number of male patrons at the establishment, ambled towards her. The light streaming in from the window behind him created a halo around his greying curls.

'Are you scared of dogs? They are completely harmless. Anton Pais,' he said, extending his hand. His accent was like a curry made from disparate leftovers. An unfamiliar flavour, half British, half Goan.

A blond man tapped him from the back. 'Welcome to paradise,' Pais said, before giving him an exuberant hug. On Leela's return, she received the same spirited greeting before Pais headed to the kitchen.

When he passed their table again, Garima asked him for the Wi-Fi password.

'Who knows,' he said.

'Is there someone else I can ask?'

He bent closer, his head in line with hers and said, 'That's the password – whoknows. No space, all small letters.'

A frizzy-haired young man joined them. Leela's newest boyfriend, Garima deduced, from the way her mother immediately nestled her head against his shoulder.

The dark shack and discordant music made her feel displaced. Her life in Bombay, grief, anger – suddenly distant notions. She bent forward, tearing pieces of buttered bread, her eyes still on Pais, and she fed his dogs.

～

The following evening, she returned to Sandcastle – an unplanned diversion from Mapusa market, where she had managed to procure a new washing machine for the house.

She made her way to the bar where Pais was pouring drinks. In the following hour, the conversation shifted from their love for Goan food to her cousin's death.

'A pot of beans was boiling on the stove when she collapsed. That's all she had done in the last few years. Cooked, cleaned, looked after her daughter. She had a law degree, you know.'

Pais replied, 'I cook every day too. Perhaps that would be a fitting end – dropping dead, my face floating in a pot of crab masala.' He seemed amused at the morbid imagery. 'So, your cousin cooked, and what do you do?'

She had trained as a physiotherapist. During her six-month internship, she was introduced to Neil at a friend's party. A year and a half later, Neil and Garima were married, had moved cities and she had turned into the oddly termed 'housewife'.

'What do I do?' Garima repeated.

Tally grocery bills. Try to bring some stability to her mother's finances, if not her life. Refrain from pushing Neil down the stairs after she had discovered the truth about his Prague trip.

She tried to find something impressive to say. Deep-sea diving. Playing the violin. But as he turned back to her with his calm, kind eyes, she told him the truth.

'I do nothing, I suppose. Nothing at all.'

Pais offered her another beer. She leaned back, cradling the cold bottle, as he took a fine sheet of paper from a red tin box and rolled the leaves inside.

On her eighth afternoon in Goa, she found herself lying beside Pais, on a creaky bed, in a room attached to the back of the shack. In the light from a bare bulb hanging over the bed, she examined her lover. Her mind running over the syllables of that newly reacquainted word. His narrow chest, his nose, chin, all ended in tightly triangulated points. She peered at the gash on his abdomen, 'A knife fight?' she asked, coming closer to stare at the keloid scar.

'Appendicitis,' he replied before they were interrupted by his dogs. They were howling in unison outside to an old Hindi song playing on Sandcastle's speakers.

'It's like your pets are trying to sing along too,' Garima said.

'They are not my pets but, yes, they love music.'

'They live here, don't they?' she asked.

'They come of their own free will and leave the same way.' He scrunched his face, lines spreading like tiny fissures around his eyes, and crooned, 'Because they don't belong to me and I don't belong to them. Do you remember this song?'

'Freedom,' she replied. She knew every George Michael song, had collected his posters as a teenager.

These were not the exact lyrics but close enough. And she knew the conversation wasn't about pets.

'You are a lot like someone I know,' she said, cutting short his discourse on dogs and ownership.

'Garima,' he answered, a gurgle of laughter tucked away in his throat, 'just don't say I remind you of your father!'

She considered telling him it was Leela, but it sounded almost incestuous.

'So, who is it – this obviously fantastic person since he seems to be my counterpart?'

'No one you know,' she said, accepting the joint he offered as she watched him pull on a pair of crumpled shorts, his customary uniform behind Sandcastle's bar.

Driving back to her mother's house, the song was stuck in her head, the way it had once played incessantly on her yellow Discman.

'Freedom, you've got to give for what you take,' she sang, humming the next few lines, unable to recall all the words.

Like Pais, Leela too had once unveiled her version of freedom. It was the time when Garima had accompanied her mother and grandmother to Rishikesh to submerge her grandfather's ashes into the Ganga.

In a memorable incident, only partly due to the sweater-wearing goat chewing on her grandmother's slipper, her mother had instigated an argument. This was uncharacteristic as Leela usually avoided confrontations. Garima wondered if it was grief or whether Leela had been on something, uppers, downers, whatever she used to take in those days.

'Like all Sindhi women of a certain class, Mama,' Leela said, 'you believe in Sathya Sai Baba and words that begin with a capital M – Morality, Matrimony and Monogamy.'

She then turned on the twenty-three-year-old Garima, 'And you have made Garima just like you. You both are interested in constructing dams, controlling the natural flow. I am like that twig,' she said, gesticulating wildly as she spotted a branch in the polluted river. 'I want to drift along. I just want to be free.'

While her mother's disregard for convention had

always agitated her, in Pais she found it liberating. She could, for the first time, try drifting herself, without feeling the need to be the one holding an extra life jacket in her hand.

~

The following Saturday, Garima returned from Sandcastle to find Neil waiting for her on the porch.

'It took me just thirty minutes from the airport, can you believe it? I thought we would have lunch together but Leela said you had gone to the market?' His tone placed it between a statement and a question. Neil pressed on with a joviality that she supposed felt equally false to his own ears because she saw him wince. 'Doesn't matter! I anyway wanted to surprise you for your birthday. But even if I hadn't, it would still end up as a surprise because you haven't been answering my calls. I thought everything was okay now. So what is this, Garu?'

Despite Goa's humidity, Neil's polo T-shirt was crisply ironed, his deck shoes an immaculate white. He leaned forward to kiss her and she retreated, tucking her chin in a backward motion.

'You look,' he hesitated, before adding, '. . . different,' as he took in her shorts, the thin vest, her braided hair.

In all the lists Garima habitually made, involving annual goals and weekly tasks, she had not accounted for Neil's betrayal. It had been one of the other wives, Ameeta, who had discovered text messages and informed her about the escorts hired on their husbands' Prague trip. While Neil called it a mistake and sobbed on her shoulder, Garima's reaction had been clinical. Could you get Hepatitis B from oral sex, she had wondered. As if she was still working with Dr Kumble, listening to a patient's account of tearing a ligament.

A pair of crows landed on the tray laid out by her mother's housekeeper. One dipped his beak into the pot of sugar. Neil moved towards them, waving his arms, an animated scarecrow with cheeks turning red in the late afternoon sun.

She had not told Leela about Pais. But her mother must have made her own assumptions when she dropped by for a drink and spotted Garima with him at the Sandcastle bar. If Neil's arrival was meant to be an ambush, it would not surprise her if he was merely the foot soldier, and her mother, the brigadier in charge.

~

The bassist hired for her birthday party paused his discordant rendition of 'Stand by Me' at Pais's interruption. Garima could see the two men shaking hands and thumping backs. It was the first time she had seen Pais in trousers. Khaki green, paired with his dusty flip-flops.

He made his way across her mother's noisy living room and kissed her on both cheeks. Then he handed Garima a spiky-leafed plant with six closed buds and one fine-spun flower, the colour of winter sun.

The previous evening, she had informed Neil she needed a break. Two weeks in Goa and she would return to Bombay. Taking rounds of the garden, Leela had asked if this was her way of throwing a tantrum, 'with this Pais thing' as she referred to it.

'Ma, there is nothing going on between us.'

'Pais must be in a guidebook somewhere, right next to Cape d'Or and Montenegro. On a list of ten things that worthy travellers must tick off their bucket list,' Leela said with a caustic laugh. 'Two months ago, he turned his shack partly into a photography studio because of some Daisy Muller. Before that it was some Turkish girl. And someone said there is a wife too, but I am not sure,' her mother added.

It didn't matter to her. Her expectations were realistic, Garima told herself. A brief relationship without any heartache.

She sensed her husband behind her as she stood talking to Pais. Neil took the heavy planter from her hands. A brief introduction, where she thought her voice sounded strained, though neither of the men seemed to have noticed.

Pais, without the awkwardness of a man having sex with the other man's wife, enveloped Neil in a bear hug. 'Welcome to paradise,' he said, in the same rolling cadence that he greeted all the travellers who drifted through Goa.

~

Neil and Garima had a second honeymoon, or at least that is how Neil would later refer to their holiday in Mauritius. In a haze of guilt, relief and heartbreak on both sides, there had been a renewed urgency to mend their marriage.

They would snorkel before lunch, holding hands underwater, following the occasional turtle, a school of tiny blue fishes. Evenings were spent playing backgammon, having sex in each room of their villa and once in the pool. They attended the Around the World party organized by their hotel. Drinking at every pit stop that constituted a country, till they were stumbling through Russia, dancing in Indonesia and the next morning could not remember if they had been to Australia or Austria at the very end.

A new start, they promised each other, exchanging friendship bands from the hotel gift shop in lieu of rings.

This was a month after Garima's two weeks in Goa had ended early and without a warning.

Pais had told her he needed to go away for a few days and would be back by the weekend. She dropped by Sandcastle every day, conscious of the servers, ordering drinks she didn't want as an excuse to wait. He was back on Sunday with his buoyant greeting and a tight hug. When he sat beside her, a chubby boy trotted towards him and clambered on to his lap.

'Rumi, my son! He is turning four this month.'

'How nice,' she said, using the sentence as a placeholder, trying not to seem hurt that he hadn't mentioned the boy earlier.

He passed Garima a handwritten menu. Along with prawns and fried fish, there was a new list of vegan dishes. 'Rachel is altering the menu to expand our clientele,' Pais explained.

He brought Rachel over to meet her. 'His formerly estranged wife' was how the tall woman introduced herself. They laughed, Pais and her, like it was a private joke. When Pais went to the kitchen, Garima left, shuffling on gritty feet, sand wedged between her toes.

She returned home at dusk. When her mother opened the door, Garima said, 'Pais is back, with a wife. He has a son.'

'Yes, someone was telling me – wait, was it Marc … no, it was Jacinda – that his family had returned. The wife is an instructor, Kundalini yoga or something. Yoga has been twisted into all these fancy forms now. Hot yoga, Yin yoga, Power yoga, this Kundalini yoga.'

149

'Ma, stop. If you knew they were back, why didn't you tell me?'

Her mother didn't reply.

'Ma?'

'I just got to know too. And, anyway, when I say anything, you jump at my throat. Garu, Neil is a decent chap. There is a future there. Go home and work on your marriage. That's the right thing to do.'

Garima's surge of anger had a physicality. She felt it in her stomach, then it rose to her chest and flew out of her mouth.

'You are such a hypocrite! You have lived the way you like, marriages discarded, getting stoned all the time, but everyone else should always be responsible and sensible.'

'I don't do it for fun. It helps with my work.'

'Yes, drugs, art and rock and roll.'

'Half the time I don't think even you know what you are saying. Now stop this, come have some tea. I have the most fragrant jasmine tea. Kamli brought me so many flavours when she was here last month.'

'I don't drink tea. I drink coffee. You can't even remember that though you always remember what your boyfriends like, even this current idiot!'

'Don't get angry with me, I haven't done anything. And what would you end up doing with Pais anyway in the long run?'

Her mother patted her on the head, the familiar dried paint on her fingers, abrasive and comforting at the same time. 'You know, you had a green sweater that got stuck in the drawer and ripped? Your grandmother embroidered a star over the hole. I remember how much you ended up wearing it. Some things are worth mending, that's all I am saying. Go back, Garu. Whatever happens, happens for the best.'

In hindsight, it was perhaps the only piece of sensible advice her mother had given her.

Leela as a mother. Leela as a grandmother. If Garima charted these two points on a graph, the first half would resemble an electrocardiogram. Jagged peaks and troughs. The line would then rise, as if someone was holding a rope steady at the edge of a cliff and hoisting a climber up.

Shortly after Garima had her two children, Rohan and Ishika, her mother left Goa for Les Baux-de-

Provence with Hugo, her third husband. Every winter, she would visit her grandchildren in Bombay with bags of toys and sweets. During the summer holidays, she insisted the family come to her. Garima would pack straw hats, bug spray, linen shirts and swimsuits, the masala banana chips her mother loved and a mandatory gift for Hugo.

In the garden adjoining the small cottage with Hugo's figurative sculptures scattered between olive trees, Garima would often find Leela and Ishika sitting on the patchy grass, their heads close together, immersed in splattering paint over primed canvases. Her mother would play video games with Rohan. Their gamer names were almost identical. Leela saw this as a sign of their bond. 'I think he wanted to be Rodin, like me,' she said, 'but since he still mirrors some letters, he accidentally typed in Robin.'

When Neil teased her about turning into a doting grandmother, she added, 'It's easier with your grandchildren. The generational gap is wide enough so we can stretch out our arms without smacking each other in the face.'

This was the summer when Rohan got splinters

lodged in his bottom. The seven-year-old had been sitting on one of Hugo's unfinished works.

Hugo, his amiable expression displaced by an irate frown, accused Rohan of cracking the foundation plank. Garima was pulling the splinters out with a tweezer as Rohan cried, and Hugo continued circling them, muttering in French. When Leela, hearing the commotion, emerged from her studio, Garima thought she would reprimand Rohan. Art was a sanctified business in her mother's household. Instead, she sat down beside her grandson and dismissed Hugo with an impatient wave.

'He's a child, Hugo, and you should stop acting like one,' she said, before wiping her grandson's tears with one of the stained rags she always carried in her pocket.

⁓

In the schmaltzy movies Garima had seen, there was always a grand cathartic moment. Mistakes admitted. Forgiveness distributed. Teary reunions against a sweeping soundtrack. With Leela and her, the closest they had come to a resolution was just before Garima fell ill.

During the last week of their summer break, Leela had taken the children to see the Arles Amphitheatre. Trying to stay out of Hugo's way, Garima decided to go into the garage and organize the boxes and cartons her mother had shipped over to France but never opened.

There was a faded rug. Mismatched crockery. A heap of yellowing notepads with sketches and photographs stapled on to frayed edges. One was of a picture of a macaw above another drawing of it, this time with a woman's face. Lines written, scratched, rewritten. Describing dreams, poems, paintings. She stumbled on to a sketch of three people in a bed. Outlines. A large figure that could be a man. A woman with a rounded belly and thick thighs, like all the women Leela painted. A child lying between them. On the other side of the page her mother had written a note.

A child to use as a bridge or a wedge. Placed in between, a breathing, living overpass that sometimes wets the bed. If it has been a day where we have clashed, then I turn on my side, using her body as a shield.

On better days, I turn to him. Last night, after a kick, because she twirls in her sleep, a gymnast trying out somersaults, I looked over, across her tiny body. He was awake. I reached out and our hands met. We watched her chest move, the way marriages do, rhythmically, up and down.

She put the book aside. Sorting the others in a chronological pile. After dinner, when they were alone, she gave Leela the notebook.

'Is that why you had me, to use me as a bridge and a wedge?

Her mother traced the figures with her stained nails.

'How can you think like that, Garu? I know you keep saying I didn't do this or that, but I did the best I could. Like you will do your best.' Then Leela let out her warbling laugh. 'And, let me tell you, whatever you do, the kids will grow up, go to therapy and end up blaming you.'

Garima wanted to ask about the man in the drawing. Her father. But she knew she would not get any answers. And she understood. There were things she could not talk about either.

⁓

Garima, returning to Goa after fifteen years, found it altered. Shards of glass, scraps of tarpaulin, initially mistaken for bluebottles and jellyfish, glistened on the sand. She propped her feet on a stool as Neil and Rohan, armed with a frisbee, headed to the beach.

After her mother's tenants had moved out last year, they had finally found a buyer for the house. But the previous owner's son had threatened to halt the sale. Rebello claimed that the deeds were still in his father's name and had never been transferred to Leela. It was Neil's suggestion to come to Goa, meet the man and reach a settlement.

'Thank God I got out before all these tourists descended here,' Leela said as she looked out at the crowded beach.

'Didn't Hugo also come here as a tourist, Ma? You shouldn't be so disparaging since you married one.'

'You know, I don't like that term, Garu.'

'What? Tourist?'

'No. Married.'

Her third marriage, Leela still claimed, was a formality to obtain a residence permit.

'There is too much weight for me in that word. Bondage and submission, but accompanied by vanilla

156

sex most of the time,' Leela had declared at a recent family gathering. 'Some people like the torture, like Madhu' – she pointed at her younger sister – 'and, of course, our Savitri here – Garu.'

Remnants of the mythological tales she had heard from her grandmother still lingered in Garima's mind. Shravana the boy who carried his parents in a basket. And Savitri, whom Leela had compared her to, who convinced the God of Death to return her husband's soul.

In her case, the roles had been reversed. Neil took on Savitri's part, as they went from one specialist to another, looking for boons against Garima's autoimmune hepatitis. Fortunately, they found one that pushed the disease into remission.

Early mornings, wearing striped pyjamas, his glasses perched on his nose, Neil sat in their living room, working on his laptop. His eyes magnified by the heavy lenses, widened further, seeing his daughter bounding down the staircase. His eyes lit up for Garima too. Not like the headlights, she teased him, that he reserved for Ishika and Rohan, but with a gentler joy.

And she had her mother. Leela had not let her spend a single night alone at the hospital.

Leela wouldn't admit that she had returned to look after her either. She claimed she wanted a change of weather. As if people visited Bombay for its two seasons – hot and damp, and hot and wet.

Leela, who had clambered down to the beach to take pictures, spotted him first.

'Pais,' Garima heard Leela call out. Garima could see hugs being exchanged and Pais thumping Neil on the back before their game restarted. The frisbee whizzed between the three, as her mother stood on the side.

He had not noticed Garima. A relief. She looked emaciated. Her skin, the colour of peeled-back corncobs because of the hepatitis. Pais had not changed much. Though his hairline had receded. Since she had not seen it occurring incrementally, it seemed more an effect of the moon than time. Robust waves pulled back to reveal vast stretches during low tide.

When Leela returned to the porch, she was quiet.

'It's . . . there is such a strong resemblance,' her mother said finally.

An unconscious nod, before Garima held herself still. She recalled sitting on the edge of the bathtub, trying to work out the exact week. Then it had finally come to her, in a burst of yellow, tecoma flowers. Pais had given her the spiky-leafed plant for her birthday in January. Rohan was an October-born Libra. The baby was born two weeks before the due date. Was he early, or was he right on time?

Her eyes darted between Pais and her son. They both had a bounding, lurching way of moving. Curly mops. One thinning, all grey, the other a dark brown. Shoulders and hips enclosed within parallel lines. Her son, unlike Neil, would not age into a jowly, fleshy man.

They had always used protection. One afternoon, the condom had slipped off. 'Stopped in time,' Pais had said. She held on to that assurance. Any misgivings, when she discovered she was pregnant after the Mauritius trip, had been firmly pushed away.

Five years after Rohan was born, though the family declared that he had her droopy eyes and Neil's complexion, she had not been as certain. There was a resemblance. She could see it even then.

Neil walked up to the porch and Garima wanted to rush to him, hold his hand, cry.

'You need anything?' he asked, patting her arm.

She could see the concern in his face. Feel it trickling down his hands when he sat holding her swollen feet in the evenings, pressing them as if they were balls of dough that could be kneaded flat.

Garima opened the pill bottle by her side and swallowed her evening dose, fighting the urge to tell him. Then it would begin. DNA tests and long discussions.

'All okay?' Neil asked.

'It just has an unpleasant aftertaste,' she said, as Neil handed Leela a beer, taking two back to the beach.

Her mother tried again, 'You don't think they look alike? When was it, Garima? That mess with Neil? It was after I finished touring with Feroz's exhibition, so it was around 2002, I think.' A fishing rod of a sentence.

She wanted to confide in her mother. For advice and absolution. She was silent, recalling her mother's advice all those years ago. 'It's like scarfing down a carton of ice cream and, unable to stomach it, you throw up on someone else.'

It was time to divert and deflect. 'Ma, the things you think of! What you are referring to was seventeen

160

years ago! You do remember that your grandson is fifteen?'

Leela pursed her lips, like she was sucking on an invisible straw. Unlike Garima, who never forgot birthdays, her mother was terrible with dates.

Garima doubled down. 'Wait, let me call Ishika and tell her what nonsense goes on inside your head.'

'Stop it, Garu!' Leela said. 'As it is you tell the children rubbish stories about me. "Oh look, the flaky granny who wanted to auction her car on Twitter!"'

A surrender or an unspoken pact, she wondered, as Leela lapsed into silence, sipping on her beer.

The sea deepened to a stubbed-out ash grey as Garima waited on the porch beside her mother. She watched the frisbee fly between the two men and her beautiful, bright boy. Soon it would be too dark to play.

Jelly Sweets

The jelly sweets needed guarding. Arranged in tin trays on the terrace, the sugar-speckled gelatin attracted hordes of flies. When they set, Abba would chop the sheets into perfect squares and stack the gem-like sweets in glass jars at the shop.

It was Nusrat's turn that afternoon. She was meant to ward off the flies with a crumpled paper fan but it had started drizzling. Abba would be livid if the trays got drenched. Pulling her dupatta over her head, she began carrying the trays towards the stairwell.

Amma often lectured Nusrat and her two sisters for getting their hair wet. 'This is how you girls get lice in your hair,' she would say, 'and then I have to sit for hours and take them out.'

Nusrat and Mubeena, the quieter ones, would nod in agreement, but Afshan, the eldest, once snapped back, 'Amma, sometimes you say "if you don't wash your hair you will get lice". Now you say "you will get lice because it is wet". You tell us, how can we wash our hair without getting it wet?'

On the adjacent terrace, Fayyaz was standing with his sons, pulling kurtas and shirts off the clothes line. In all the years they had been neighbours, Nusrat had rarely seen Fayyaz idle. He always had something in his hands. Either his account book – where he recorded the size of his daily catch – novels and sketchbooks, or even blocks of wood that he whittled into toys.

When they were younger, Fayyaz would hop over the central parapet to join the sisters for a game of gutte. His shy smile would deepen when the sisters offered him sweets. He always picked the green ones from the tin trays.

Fayyaz's marriage brought his wife, Shaguna, into their lives. Cheerful and outgoing, she had befriended all three sisters. Her sudden death from malaria the previous year had come as a shock. Abba had spoken to the panchayat, urging them to spray kerosene and DDT over the drains and stagnant pools in the village, but nothing had been done.

These days, Fayyaz came up to the terrace only with his four-year-old twins. Though he still greeted her, he didn't ask for sweets or cross over to show Nusrat his carvings.

From the landing below, Amma called out, 'Come down, Nusrat! Afshan is getting Mubeena ready and you have to help me in the kitchen.'

It was meant to be a big day. A boy was coming to see Mubeena, all the way from Bombay.

～

That evening, a resigned Tahir Bhai sat alone with his second tumbler of whisky, a papad on the side. The family had finally given up waiting for their guest to arrive.

Despite Tahir Bhai's desire for a son to carry on the legacy of 'Samji and Sons', fate had dealt him three daughters. After Afshan and Mubeena were born, he had consulted a blind mystic hoping for the long-awaited male heir. It had been an unsuccessful attempt. Mumtaz wept when Nusrat was born, and

Tahir Bhai, faced with a third daughter, started hitting the bottle and had been getting knocked out in return ever since.

He was already inebriated when Mumtaz returned to the living room after changing out of her festive clothes. 'Who do these Rahimtoolas think they are? Making us waste all this time, effort and your special kachoris,' she said. 'They must have just decided that we are not good enough for their family. But they could have at least sent a message with a polite excuse like some relative's death or an accident.'

Tahir Bhai nodded, his words slurring as he replied, 'You are right; people don't realize that the first rule of civility is the necessity of telling lies.'

Mubeena, listening to the conversation as her mother undid her braids, interrupted her parents. 'Amma, what if something happened to him? What if he really had an accident?'

'They must have just changed their mind. Let me tell you, if something happened had to him, we would have heard about it.' Though Mumtaz didn't say it, she was relieved that the suitor had not shown up. Mubeena looked like a clown. She shouldn't have entrusted Afshan with getting her younger daughter ready.

Afshan, unlike her sisters, had not inherited their mother's grey eyes and clear complexion. She was made aware of this in different ways. Just the previous week, their masi, patting each sister on the cheek, had said, 'Mumtaz, your younger two are just like you, your copy, so lovely – mashallah! The elder one is, of course, ditto Tahir Bhai.'

Since the most remarkable features her father possessed were a hooked nose and beady eyes, this was not a compliment. Masi must have realized that her words could be considered unkind because she quickly added, 'But, you know, they say that girls who look like their father are very lucky.'

Disgruntled that a boy was coming to see the younger Mubeena, when, as the eldest, it should have been her turn, Afshan had drenched her sister's hair with oil and had braided it into two plaits. She had then taken their mother's kohl and drawn two thick lines around Mubeena's eyes.

When Mumtaz finally saw Mubeena, she hurriedly got her daughter to wash her face. There was not much that could be done about the oily braids and the poor girl still had dark remnants of the kohl under her swollen eyes.

The doorbell rang after dinner. The Samji women darted in different directions as Tahir Bhai, already passed out on the couch, remained oblivious. Afshan, banished to her room, clambered down the stairs in her nightclothes. Mumtaz pulled Mubeena into the kitchen, trying to twist her oily hair into a bun. Nusrat crossed the living room and opened the main door.

'Ya Ali Madad,' said the tired-looking young man standing on the porch, 'I am Abdul, Iqbal Rahimtoola's son. Sorry, I'm so late.'

The khichda was almost done. It didn't quite match Abba's but the flavours reminded her of home. Despite moving to Bombay almost a decade ago, home, in Nusrat's mind, was still Satpati.

She gave it a quick stir, added more lemon juice and scooped half a teaspoon of the broken wheat, lentil and meat mixture on to her palm. The meat was tender, the lentil base delicately spiced with just the right amount of cumin and cardamom.

Abdul wandered into the kitchen, asking if she

had seen his striped shirt. Taking the spoon from her hand, he dipped it into the khichda, raised it to his lips for a taste and returned it to the pot. Nusrat reached out. Placing her hand on his arm, she said, 'Don't make it jhoota.'

Abdul shrugged off her hand. 'Stop all this village talk! Do you know, there isn't even a word for "jhoota" in English? The closest translation would be "tainting something with your saliva". Would you consider what I'm doing as tainting your precious khichda?' His annoyance at her traditional ways often simmered beneath his casual demeanour, but he would never reveal that aspect to his friends. Instead, he preferred to spin the tale of their marriage as 'an arranged love affair straight out of a movie'.

At dinner parties, he liked recounting the serendipitous events that led to their marriage. 'My 11 a.m. train from Bombay to Palghar left on time,' he would begin. 'Then a buffalo wandered on to the tracks, and the train collided with it. I probably should've turned back, but something inside me urged me onward to Satpati. And thank goodness I did because fate, in the form of my beautiful wife, met me at the doorstep.'

He omitted the practical considerations that had influenced his decision. From among the three sisters – one with puffy, raccoon-like smeared eyes, the other, a lanky dishevelled figure draped in a worn-out nightgown and Nusrat, with her refined features and pleasant manner – he had picked the most presentable option.

Abdul dipped the spoon back into the khichda and said, 'Let's not take the whole batch to the Jamaat. We can save some for our visit to Bipin's tonight.'

Nusrat's lips tightened and she focused on the condiments she was preparing. She always felt uneasy at these gatherings. Initially, she had tried speaking in Kutchi with Bipin and Salima, a Khoja couple who were part of Abdul's tight-knit group of friends. But she had struggled to keep up with the English that peppered their conversations.

Over time, Nusrat had learned to follow their swift exchanges, nodding and smiling when necessary, but confidence still eluded her. She refrained from speaking at these gatherings unless it was absolutely necessary. It was only during their light-hearted games, a ritual Abdul claimed they'd carried from their college days, that she was forced to participate.

They would pose absurd questions to each other like, 'If Mushtaq were a superhero, what would be his name?' The friends would invent outlandish monikers and burst into fits of laughter. When it was her turn, she tried to keep it simple and disappear into the background as quickly as possible.

Once, Salima, savouring Nusrat's mirchi ka salan, continued the game with, 'Chalo, let's try this one. If Nusrat won a lottery, what would she do?'

Abdul, quick-witted as always, replied, 'She would leave me and run away with Dev Anand.'

The group turned their attention to Nusrat, waiting for her response. Uncertain of what to say, she hesitated, before saying, 'Clap!'

Laughter erupted, but she couldn't shake off the feeling that she had been the subject of their amusement.

Nusrat had always been soft-spoken, but her marriage to Abdul seemed to deepen her introversion. Timid was the word her sisters used to describe her now, and she couldn't help but agree.

Even in the bustling jamaatkhana, after prayers, when the hall would come alive with laughter and chatter, she kept to herself. Her interactions with the other women were limited to the mandatory Shah-jo-Deedar, that required her to exchange greetings with the people sitting beside her.

It was only while holding her son's tiny hand that she felt a flicker of strength. When she introduced Sabu to others, she nudged him forward, watching him with a mix of indulgence and pride as they pinched his cheeks.

As she stirred the pot, Sabu's tiny face, complete with his pointy chin, flooded her thoughts. She had teased him the night before that he looked like an old man with his two missing front teeth.

'Sabu Miyan, please practise smiling with your mouth closed for the photograph. Like this,' she had demonstrated, hoping he would follow suit. Abdul had promised they would get portraits taken at Patel Bhai's studio on Sabu's upcoming birthday. It would be the first time they would pose for photographs together as a family.

Sabu looked up from her lap, grinning toothily. 'Like this?'

'No, my little kuchlu-puchlu. We will practise in front of the mirror tomorrow. Now, close your eyes. We have time for only two stories tonight. It's getting late.'

'Amma, three stories. Please!'

This nightly ritual held a special place in their lives. Sabu would lie down with his head in her lap, holding on to his precious stuffed donkey with one hand while Nusrat told him stories. That night, she started with the adventures of the clever monkey and then told him a story about the antics of a foolish crow. Like every other night, Sabu asked for the story about Nasreddin Hodja.

'Amma, tell me again why Hodja refused to write letters for his neighbour?'

'Because his handwriting was so terrible.'

'Just like mine, Amma?'

'Listen to the story first. Let me see . . . yes, Hodja claimed he couldn't write the letter because he simply didn't have the time to go all the way to Baghdad. He feared that, if he wrote it, he'd have to make the journey himself once the letter reached its destination. You see, his handwriting was so bad that only he could decipher it. Yes, it resembled yours, Sabu Miyan.'

In her letters to her sisters, Nusrat tried to capture the sense of contentment she felt with Sabu nestled in her lap, her fingers gently stroking his hair as he drifted off to sleep. But she never found the words for what she felt and instead filled the pages with news of him – a clever thing he had said that had made the family laugh or his naughty antics.

Sabu would turn seven soon. Nusrat had been saving up to purchase several gifts for his birthday. Abdul, who indulged him equally, would not mind that instead of one present she was planning on giving him four, but her mother-in-law, Bibi Jaan, often chided her over spoiling Sabu with unnecessary treats. Nusrat had already devised a plan – if his grandmother asked, she would simply say the gifts were from her Abba.

⁓

The glass prayer beads glittered in the sunlight. Nusrat's fingers moved feverishly over them as she watched Sabu being lowered into the shallow grave.

'Baji, come and sit here. Have some water.' Abdul's niece offered, but Nusrat barely heard her, staring instead at the mukhi holding up a handful of mud. The hollow pit where her son's body had been placed appeared to be double his size. The diggers must not have known it was a child's burial. Unsure if the scriptures allowed it, Nusrat had placed the small grey donkey beneath the flowers covering her son's body.

She had been watching Sabu from the bedroom window, the one that faced east and was opened at the break of dawn. Her son did not enjoy cricket as much as he liked playing chor–police. Still, every Saturday morning he would rush barefoot to join the other boys in the compound, with his mother often following behind, clutching his slippers or a half-finished glass of milk.

When the ball struck him, he didn't cry. He just stood there. His friends claimed his last words were, 'See where you are throwing, stupid!' By the time Nusrat had run down the stairs and reached the playground, he had fallen to the ground.

Meaningless words echoed like buzzing cicadas around her. A cousin speaking of her husband's death. An elderly man telling her father-in law, 'Aziz Niazi, you know, the cricketer, he also died like this, after being hit by a ball. He had played eight first-class matches for Karachi.'

As if someone else's loss was a balm that could be applied over another's pain.

~

Day after day, Nusrat stared at the building compound. She sat by her bedroom window, searching for a moment that would never return. She saw the ball arcing through the air. She heard the resounding impact on a body, a hard knock. Though, on that day, she had not heard any sound.

She pictured her body falling, all the way down, till she joined her son on the ground. It would hurt for a minute but then it would all stop. She climbed on to the ledge. The sleeves of her kurta fluttered like the parrots who landed on the wired poles across the street.

Hands pulled her back. The window slammed shut. But she could still see the body lying on the ground below.

~

This time, the journey from Bombay to Satpati proved uneventful, and it marked Abdul's final trip to the small fishing village.

Standing at the threshold where he had first seen his wife, Abdul felt increasingly trapped when Mumtaz began sobbing and asked him to reconsider his decision.

He tried explaining to his mother-in-law. 'And what if Nusrat does it when I am not there? This is the third time she has tried to jump. If she succeeds, then who will be blamed? The whole community will point fingers at us saying we did not take care of her.'

'Beta, I request you with folded hands, please don't do this. Your Abba said the same things to Tahir, but I wanted to talk to you.' Mumtaz wiped her leaking nose with the back of her hand and continued, 'Nusrat is your wife; go speak to her, you can make this all right. Talaq is a big step. In our whole family, this has never happened. Just think of her – after this, what will happen to her?'

'How am I supposed to speak to her when she doesn't talk to anyone?! Fourteen months and not one word has come out of Nusrat's mouth since the funeral.'

He couldn't explain to his mother-in-law that the loss of his son had left behind a blinding rage along with a guilt-ridden desire to move on. He wanted to take his wife, catch her by the shoulders and shake her out of her grief. That there were nights when desperation and, yes, anger made him lift Nusrat's sari and push inside her dryness, to evoke a response, a sound, even if it was one of pain.

They had tried hakims, doctors and had even taken her to the famous Baba Yatim. The healer had thrown a handful of ash on Nusrat. The only change consisted of coins emerging from Abdul's pocket and going into the donation plate.

Stepping back from the door, Abdul said, 'We have tried everything. Nusrat needs your care. She needs her mother.' Then he added, 'Also, out of decency and respect for Tahir Bhai, Abba has sent the mahr,' as if hoping it would absolve him of his responsibility.

Abdul's father had disagreed, believing they were not obligated to hand over the contractual dowry. In his view, the marriage had broken due to Nusrat's actions. 'We were eight of us. My Ammi lost two children. She didn't go mad like this. She didn't behave as if someone had cut her tongue off or started jumping out of windows,' he told Abdul.

Bibi Jaan, who had spent years looking for clues of her daughter-in-law's ineptitude as a homemaker, was surprisingly staunch in her defence. Outnumbered, she insisted that the least they could do was send Nusrat back with two trunks, packed with everything she had brought with her.

~

Mumtaz nudged Nusrat forward as they made their way through the crowd at Vallabhbhai Patel Stadium. Led by Tahir Bhai, in his best sherwani, the family had arrived in Bombay for the coronation of Aga Khan IV. It was also a family reunion, prompted by an invitation from Afshan and her husband, Karim, who were attending the ceremony along with Muni, their two-year-old daughter.

A year after Nusrat was married, Afshan had unexpectedly received a proposal from a well-connected family from Hyderabad. Mumtaz liked taking credit for her eldest daughter's successful match. 'It is only due to all my prayers. You know when we went to the Ajmer Sharif Dargah, I tied a thread for Afshan specially,' she boasted to her relatives.

Passing the pipers and drummers entering the stadium, they settled into their seats. Mumtaz patted Afshan, pleased with their proximity to the stage. 'Left to your father, we would be sitting on the floor on the other side of the fence like all those people. If luck favours us, even the Rahimtoolas will see us right here in the front.'

Two years had passed since they heard that Abdul had remarried. Within months of leaving Nusrat at Satpati, Abdul had obtained permission from the mukhi and the council, dissolving the previous marriage. After that, he had wasted no time in finding another wife.

The coronation proceedings unfolded on stage. The Aga Khan, in an embroidered coat, was already sitting on a grand throne but Afshan was unable to concentrate on the ceremony. She kept looking at Nusrat instead. Her sister appeared as sickly as before, with no signs of improvement.

Karim invited the Samjis out to dinner that evening. Despite the prohibition, Tahir Bhai had managed to smuggle in a flask of whisky which was discreetly poured into teacups.

During the elaborate meal, discussions grew heated, especially concerning why Prince Aly had been bypassed in favour of his son as the next Aga Khan. Afshan, unable to hold back, finally spoke out. 'Stop making excuses, Abba. Everyone knows that Prince Aly is a playboy.'

Amma with a puzzled frown asked, 'But, what is a playboy? Is it like a cowboy? I knew he liked horses, but that's no reason to remove him from the line of succession.'

While Afshan laughed, her sister remained silent. She had repeatedly tried involving Nusrat in the conversation, only to be met with a nod or a shake of her head. Afshan noticed the trembling spoon in Nusrat's frail hands. Her food remained untouched on the plate. There were small patches on Nusrat's scalp where her hair had fallen out.

What troubled Afshan more was that her sister's silence seemed to have led her family to behave as if she were deaf as well. They communicated with her through gestures whenever they needed food passed or water poured. It was not out of unkindness; just carelessness.

As the bill arrived and Tahir Bhai perfunctorily wrestled with his son-in-law before allowing him to pay, Afshan's uneasiness over her sister's condition deepened.

She had often wished she could trade places with Nusrat, even cursed fate for favouring her less than her sister. And now poor Nusrat had lost everything – her husband, her son, and her voice. It would not be easy but she would persuade Karim into letting her stay back in Satpati with Muni for a few months.

⁓

It's all empty. These were the words that Nusrat eventually wrote down. Nusrat could not speak but no one had checked if she could communicate in any other way. Afshan gave her a notebook and at first coaxed, then badgered her into writing. 'Write anything, Nusrat – it doesn't matter what. Write Afshan is a donkey, I don't care. Whatever comes into your head,' she would tell her.

At first, Nusrat's writing consisted of a few hesitant words at a time, her faint handwriting barely leaving indentations on the lined paper. Encouraged by Afshan, she continued using the notebook.

Unlike the rest of the family, Afshan never displayed overt sympathy, nor did she allow Nusrat to be forgotten in the room. Treating her as she had during their childhood, the elder sister playfully drummed her scalp while oiling her hair, tickled her while chopping vegetables. When Amma scolded her, she brushed it off with, 'I just want to hear that funny laugh Nusrat has. You know how she sounds, like some old woman with a phlegmy cough.' Then she would hunch her back and produce a strange gurgling sound, making Muni, Amma and Afshan laugh.

Amma had planted marigolds near the windows to deter mosquitoes. Through the day, just as the marigolds reached for the sun, Nusrat found herself drawn to her elder sister. She was warmed by Afshan's relentless cheer, her meaningless prattle.

In the months following Sabu's death, Nusrat had struggled to distinguish between reality and her imagination. She had seen signs everywhere. If a crow came to the window, then it was Sabu coming to talk to her. When birds flew in a pattern across the sky, it was a signal from him. A branch moving was him waving.

The Bombay flat had been filled with his presence.

He was ringing the doorbell. He was behind the door in the kitchen. He was hiding in the bathroom.

When she tried to speak, it felt like there was a pebble lodged in her throat. She had to navigate around the obstruction, push against it repeatedly in order to get a word out. When she did, her voice emerged raspy. A feeble sound struggling to be heard. It was easier to stay silent.

Afshan arranged an appointment with a specialist in Bombay. The doctor conducted a thorough examination and diagnosed strained and tight vocal cords. 'We must free the throat,' he explained, touching her neck, 'and her chest,' he added as his fingers slid lower than required. Nusrat was given vocal exercises to stretch her throat muscles, and she managed to produce a few feeble sounds.

'I have heard of a patient in Calcutta who could not speak and, after five years, she coughed so violently that she vomited! And out it came – a button that had lodged behind her vocal cords!' The doctor laughed and added, 'But there is nothing in your throat, I can assure you. I would just tell you, push your shoulders back and massage your throat daily. We need to open up the space there and, yes, hum; practise humming every day. You know Suraiya? She came to see me during the time she was working in *Mirza Ghalib* – you have seen that one, yes? Her voice felt restricted and had lost power. I gave her the same advice and look how she sang in that movie. Superb, superb, simply superb!'

Afshan, relieved that her sister did not have a permanent physical ailment, was even more determined to break down her silence.

Every morning, the radio's crochet cover was flung aside, and the sisters would hum together. As Nusrat attempted to form words, Amma and Afshan would sing along with the songs on Radio Ceylon's 'Aap Hi Ke Geet' programme.

When a song by Suraiya would play on the radio, Afshan would sing even louder in her usual tone-deaf way and then end with an imitation of Dr Chandraramani saying, 'Superb, superb, simply superb!'

～

The summer brought its familiar rhythm to the rooftop of the Samji house. Amma's swollen knees made the ascent up the rickety staircase to the terrace a laborious task. As Nusrat's condition improved, Amma, who had been afraid to let her go anywhere unaccompanied, began to delegate tasks to her youngest. Numerous things required drying in their household: clothes, spices, pickles and sweets. Nusrat would go up and down the stairs, practising her humming, carrying buckets and laying out aluminium trays.

On the adjoining terrace, the sisters would see Fayyaz with his account books or reading old issues of *Biswin Sadi*. Lanky in his youth, the years of hauling boats to the shore and carrying heavy bundles of net had turned him into a muscular, though still lean, man. His long, weathered face, half-shadowed by a closely cropped beard, possessed a starkness that had earlier been tempered by a bashful gaze.

Fayyaz followed a routine that rarely changed. He left the house before the first light of dawn and returned from the docks late in the afternoon. Once home, he would retreat to a corner, reading or working on his accounts. His schedule was disrupted only when his boys were home from their boarding school in Poona.

Amma, with her traditional views, expressed her dissatisfaction at his decision to send the twins to an English-medium school. 'As if our schools are not good enough for his children,' she grumbled, believing in the superiority of Urdu over all languages.

Afshan defended Fayyaz's desire for a better future for his sons, saying that her daughter would also be educated in a similar system but Amma was not convinced. 'When you throw something out, like an uncomfortable chair, you don't say "let's keep the legs and throw the rest out". You toss the whole thing. With so much difficulty, we threw these English people out, but we want to keep their language, wah!'

Nusrat, recalling how often she had felt inadequate in Bombay due to her limited command of the English language, supported her sister in these battles with Amma.

As Afshan prepared to return to Hyderabad, she spoke to Amma about keeping Nusrat occupied. She suggested that her sister could start working at the shop.

Tahir Bhai was not keen on the idea. 'It is all right when the girls were helping from home, but sitting at the till? What will people say?'

'What do you think people say now?' Mumtaz asked him. 'There are rumours that Nusrat's husband left her because she is mad. Some say she was possessed. And after we are gone, what is she going to do? Afshan is right, let her help you and later she can look after the business.'

Tahir Bhai had never won an argument with his wife in all the years they had been married and he lost this one as well.

Nusrat's days fell into a comfortable cycle. Each morning, she assisted Amma with the day's chores, often singing along with the songs on the radio as she chopped and fried. Then she would set off for the shop, carrying her father's tiffin box as she made her way through the muddy village lanes.

Tahir Bhai had sent her to assist Chandu at the back of the shop with the cooking so that she wouldn't have to speak to the customers. At first, Nusrat found herself struggling to comprehend her father's methods. He seemed to throw in sugar and besan in haphazard fistfuls. Tahir Bhai insisted that the ingredients mixed in this instinctive manner gave his creations their unique flavours. 'Even a monkey can make barfi by following a recipe: two tablespoons of this and five cups of that. But our sweets, they need more than that. It's what sets us apart. Why do you think that for every wedding in Palghar we get all the orders instead of that Kamlesh Shinde, though his shop is just five minutes from the station?'

Nusrat would watch as her father instructed Chandu and note down the exact measures.

If her future lay in running the mithai shop, despite the signboard proclaiming 'Samji and Sons', she didn't want to leave anything to approximations.

It was among the boiling vats of ghee, as she added a finely chopped paste of figs and dates, or mixed delicate strands of saffron to rounded mounds of cottage cheese, a sweetmeat her father had termed Amrapali, that she began to feel surer of herself.

The steadiness of her hands and the compliments from Chandu gave her confidence. Soon she began to hear customers commenting favourably on her jaggery-glazed barfi or her kopra pak.

In the late afternoon lull, Nusrat would read books of poetry. A family friend from Lucknow had presented Tahir Bhai with his favourite detective novels and had also brought along a book of poems by Ada Jafri.

The melancholic verses struck a chord with Nusrat. Influenced by Jafri, she went as far as pinning flowers to her bun after reading her poem.

'Have wounded my hands with thorns, trying to place but one flower in my hair.'

Nusrat started copying down her favourite lines at the back of her recipe book. It was an odd compulsion, given that she already had a copy of Jafri's book. But a fear had set in, of losing her copy, leaving it out in the rain, pages coming loose.

~

Nusrat had received a letter from Afshan that morning. After laying out the setting trays, her back against the parapet, she decided to write back to her sister. Unable to still speak as clearly as she once could, she found comfort in the written form. Her handwriting was neat and well spaced. Unlike Hodja, at least I won't have to go all the way to Hyderabad to read out my letter to Afshan, she noted, as she recalled Sabu lying in her lap listening to his favourite stories.

She pushed thoughts of her son away and continued writing to her sister about Abba's recent quarrel with a customer.

A shadow blotted the page. Fayyaz was standing before her. 'I am sorry, I didn't think the sawdust would blow over this way,' he said, pointing towards one of her drying trays.

Even from a distance she could see that half the tray of jelly sweets had grit sticking to the surface. Years ago, Fayyaz had stumbled into a tray while talking to the sisters, upsetting the sweets on to the floor. Scared of Amma's legendary temper, he had begged Afshan to take the blame for the destroyed sweets.

Nusrat cut a piece out from a clean part of the tray. The jelly was pale green. Its sugar topping glistening in the sun, the edges uneven. In a voice still unpitched and hoarse, she said, 'Doesn't matter. Here, have one.'

~

As April turned into a scorching May, Nusrat and Fayyaz moved to the cooler side of the terrace under the awning. They shared sweets and occasionally stories. It was primarily Fayyaz who initiated the conversation. Usually, he told her anecdotes about the other fishermen at the Satpati docks. If a letter had arrived from Poona, then he would tell her about his mischievous boys and the number of times they were called to the principal's office.

In Fayyaz's company, Nusrat felt an easy pleasure. It was comparable to listening to the radio all by herself in the hall downstairs. She could participate as little or as much as she wanted. Nothing was required of her. With Abdul, she had always felt a constant need to be on her toes. To stretch herself, so she could meet his expectations.

Fayyaz had an endearing way of ending his anecdotes with a question, 'Right na, Nusrat?' As if his observations had been abstract concepts, only made concrete by her nodding in agreement.

One evening, a vendor called out from the narrow lane that separated their house from the sea, 'Sweet phalsa, delicious phalsa.'

Nusrat leaned over from the parapet, her sari snagging on the jagged surface. 'Sabu liked phalsa very much. There had been a thelawala who would come near our building. Depending on the season, he would have ber, phalsa, imli. Sabu would call out to him from the window, asking him to wait. He would grab my hand, and we would rush down to the gate.'

Her hand rubbing her throat, her words wobbly, like a child trying to ride a bicycle for the first time, Nusrat finally spoke about her son. She told Fayyaz about the dreams that she had after the death of her son. Sabu was sleeping next to her. Her fingers traced his cheek, marvelling at the softness. She could smell him, a milky sweetness reminiscent of glucose biscuits. Then she would wake up. For a minute, she would be unable to recall her son's face, the sound of his voice. It had terrified her. Losing fragments of him every day. She would close her eyes and try to piece together a picture of her son's face. But it would disintegrate.

'I don't have any photographs of him so I keep his clothes near me; his favourite checked shirt that had become too small, the kurta he didn't like because it was itchy. But I can't see his face clearly any longer, it all blurs now.'

Fayyaz had a photograph of Shaguna. One taken at their wedding. In the months after she had passed away, he would lie down in his bed, gazing at it. Her sharara was black and white in the picture. He knew it had been pink. He was grateful that he would always remember the way she was on the happiest day of their lives.

Fayyaz turned away from Nusrat, worried, for a moment, that she would think he was being presumptuous. He decided to go ahead, just the way he used to close his nose and jump from his father's boat into the sea, miles away from the shore.

'I am not a great artist, but I have a steady hand. If you describe him, I can try and draw his picture.'

Over the next few days, two people tried to pin down wavering images. Nusrat would often cry, where once she had been frozen, as she recalled her son's smile. They worked together, heads close to each other, with Fayyaz drawing and erasing lines.

'I think his chin was not so wide.' '. . . yes, his eyes were just like mine, they also drooped at the outer corners.'

Fayyaz looked at Nusrat carefully and rendered her eyes into her son's portrait.

The boy in the picture didn't look exactly the way she remembered her son. The cheeks were rounder and the forehead not as broad. It was enough. She had the portrait framed, and cleared a space on her dresser, propping it next to her enamelled box of pins. Before she went to bed, she would look at the drawing, at Sabu's cleft, his eyes. She gazed at her son's curly hair, parted at the side, neat, the way it used to be when he would leave for school. She could also see Fayyaz's kindness in those lines, a gentle shadow beneath the image of her son.

⌒

One winter evening, Fayyaz was late coming up to the terrace. He had gone for a meeting at the Satpati Fishermen's Society to resolve a dispute. Two fishermen had rammed their boats together in the middle of an altercation. The society, founded by a freedom fighter, had Fayyaz as a loyal member. 'Abba was content with the way things were, but I was not. How could we be happy with the prices we were being offered? When Narayan Bhai said we would start our own cooperative, I thought it was the best thing that could happen to all of us,' Fayyaz said as he handed over two plump pomfrets to Nusrat.

Sometimes he would give her two whole daras from his catch, sometimes Bombay duck. Once, as a joke, he got her a cardboard box that contained three eels. When Nusrat opened her present, one slippery fish plopped on to her foot. She mistook it for a snake and dropped the parcel in fright.

Fayyaz had three boats, but with the cost of transport to Bombay, where the fish was auctioned, and commissions to middlemen, he had just been getting by. This changed when Hussain Baig, an auctioneer from Crawford Market, came to Satpati. He struck a deal with Fayyaz. He would advance him production credit at no interest before the fishing season. In return, Fayyaz's entire catch could only be sold through him. Fayyaz used the advance to expand his business and, along with buying two additional galhat boats, he bought the first mechanized boat in all of Satpati.

Mumtaz had noticed the deepening friendship between her daughter and Fayyaz but had not pushed the matter further. A chance conversation with her tailor made Mumtaz alter her approach. While taking her measurements, he informed her, 'Your neighbour is in demand, now that he is doing so well. Even Husna is willing to ignore the fact that he is a widower with two sons. She is looking for someone to talk to him about her daughter.'

Returning from the market, Mumtaz began badgering Tahir Bhai. 'Someone else will put their foot in the door and we will be left standing outside. You talk to him today.'

Tahir Bhai was pacing up and down the lane when he spotted Fayyaz coming towards the house. Waving out to him, he exclaimed, 'Arre, Fayyaz! Everyone is talking about your new boat. Well done! Your father – Allah bless his soul – would have been so proud.'

He paused and then, aided by the two drinks he had consumed earlier, blurted out, 'Look, what I want to say to you is very practical. You need a mother for your sons. Nusrat's husband has also remarried. No one can object to this. And, one more thing, we just have to break two walls and along with our families, both our houses will also become one.'

The nikah began with the recitation of ayats at the jamaatkhana. Nusrat, wearing Amma's wedding sari with the brocade blouse that had been altered to fit her small frame, sat beside Fayyaz on the floor. The mukhi read aloud the marriage contract and after getting Nusrat's and Fayyaz's consent, began his duas. When he finished, the congregation of twenty people, including Fayyaz's twins, responded by saying 'ameen' in unison. The mukhi blessed the rings and slipped them on to Nusrat's and Fayyaz's fingers.

The day after his conversation with Tahir Bhai, Fayyaz had come to the shop. His hair was rumpled and he smelled of briny docks and engine oil. He had a pencil wedged behind one ear like he was a carpenter instead of a fisherman.

If Fayyaz had spoken about emotions or had romantic ideas, she didn't know how she would have responded. Instead, he repeated what Amma had told her – they were both alone and would benefit from each other's support.

As he sat on the bench reserved for waiting customers, she was equally clear with him. 'Amma keeps saying she is so happy for me, but I am not sure what it means to be happy any more.'

His eyes fixed on the dusty lane in front of the mithai shop, he had replied, 'I know.'

After the ring ceremony, Tahir Bhai invited the guests to the Samji house. Surrounded by her relatives, Amma and her Ajmer Sharif Dargah thread once again took credit for this match. Tahir Bhai also outdid himself by serving all the jalebi and kaju katli he had left over from the previous day's Raksha Bandhan specials.

～

A four-poster bed with a mosquito net dominated Fayyaz's bedroom. She had seen his room when the sisters used to come over to visit Shaguna. Nusrat had memories of the young woman with her easy smile and shining eyes showing them all the alterations she had made to the house after her marriage to Fayyaz.

Aside from the addition of the mosquito nets in all the rooms, the house seemed unchanged. The curtains were still the same paisley print that Shaguna had chosen, faded now and in need of repair. When she opened the bottom drawer of the dresser in the bedroom, she saw a box of pins, a half-used bottle of oil, a small handheld mirror.

She didn't ask Fayyaz to change the curtains his dead wife had selected, or empty the dresser. She was used to living with ghosts.

Fayyaz and she slipped into a comfortable routine. Both would meet after work – her husband leaving for the dock when she was still asleep – chatting about their day over dinner. She discovered that, unlike Abdul, Fayyaz was satisfied with simply prepared vegetables but it was sweets that were his weakness. A few times a week, Nusrat would bring back different delicacies for him to try from the shop.

One evening, she brought back raskadam. She had made the round balls with an outer layer of sweetened khoya and a filling of rasgulla for a special order and had some left over. Fayyaz took a bite and, his mouth still full, said, 'This is a Bengali sweet, right? Shaguna and I had gone to Calcutta to visit her chacha and she forced me to–' before halting abruptly.

'It's fine to talk about her,' Nusrat said. 'After Sabu was gone, no one spoke to me about my son. Maybe they thought I would get upset, but it hurt more that everyone behaved like he had never existed.'

As they both sat at the table with moist eyes, she noted the difference between people who had suffered deep, unexpected loss and those who had been fortunate enough to see it from a distance. The former didn't console each other. They were aware that grief was permanent; you just got used to living with the empty space that had been left behind.

Marriage brought another change. Along with becoming accustomed to another person lying beside her at night, Nusrat had to get used to inhabiting her body again. All these years, her skin and limbs had felt distant, like an acquaintance that you occasionally ran into at the market. Now she felt an awareness of the texture of her arms, the sensitive spots on her nape. She started using the Charmis cream that Afshan had bought her. Her fingers lingering across her forearms as she rubbed the cream in.

The other unexpected gift was Fayyaz's gratitude. He had become so settled in doing things himself that when she ironed his clothes or put balm on his temples, he would tell her, with a smile, 'You are spoiling me too much.'

Fayyaz had started travelling to Bombay once a week. He would make rounds of the fish market as he slowly learned the ropes of the export trade. He once told Nusrat, 'They all have crooked scales and even the honest ones get offended if you don't offer a bribe.'

One evening, after he returned from Bombay, he said that he had spoken to Hussain about Samji and Sons. 'Dinshaw Irani's trucks anyway take our fish to the market – why don't we send shipments of mithai, and farsan with that? Hussain is keen to open a store in partnership.'

Tahir Bhai was hesitant at first but Nusrat convinced Amma that it could be a successful enterprise. She started accompanying Fayyaz on his weekly trips. The stationmaster, aware that 'Fayyaz saab and his missus', as he referred to them, boarded the 10 a.m. train every Monday, would delay the train's departure on the rare occasion when they were late.

On one visit, Fayyaz suggested that they spend the night in Bombay. He booked a room at a small hotel near the station. It was only after they finished paying that they realized their room was on the seventh floor and the hotel did not have a lift.

After walking up four flights, Fayyaz noticed that Nusrat was getting breathless. He insisted that he would carry her the rest of the way up. On reaching the next landing, Nusrat saw that Fayyaz's face was turning red and he was panting. Despite his protests, she stopped him and they both sat on the wooden steps. She tried explaining to him that his sense of protectiveness was excessive, making light of it by saying, 'You sometimes behave as if I am a puri that will deflate with one poke.'

He was quiet for a few moments and then said, 'If I worry about you too much then, perhaps, it is because there was a time I wish I had done more.'

She knew that Fayyaz carried the guilt of relying on the village hakim instead of taking Shaguna to a hospital. She reached for his arm and they sat holding hands till he caught his breath.

Afshan returned to Satpati the following summer with her daughter and two suitcases filled with gifts for the family. Nusrat had written to her about her pregnancy. Though her sister was in her fourth month, it was difficult to tell under the voluminous kurtas she favoured.

Afshan soon discovered that what her parents had proposed as a pragmatic arrangement between Fayyaz and Nusrat had turned into a deep connection.

Even their family business, Samji and Sons, reflected the change. The dusty, neglected air that had enveloped the sweet shop when Tahir Bhai had been in charge had been cast away now that Nusrat had taken over. Her sister returned from work by five-thirty in the evening. She would rush to the kitchen, especially if the twins were down during their holidays. Switching the radio on, she would hum along as she cooked. Just after 7 p.m., Nusrat would wash her hands thoroughly. She would rub lemon on her fingers and apply drops of attar before Fayyaz reached home.

Through the summer, Afshan observed the two of them. Their heads bent together, their bodies unconsciously mirroring each other. The way they touched each other on the shoulder or the back when they crossed paths from the living room to the kitchen.

One evening, Fayyaz returned home early. As the family gathered before dinner, he asked Nusrat teasingly to guess what he had brought her.

'It has to be fish, what else!' she said, shaking her head.

'Yes, that's exactly what I got you.' Fayyaz lifted Nusrat's hand and gave her a pair of gold earrings. Two small pomfrets, their scales finely etched, gleamed in the centre of her palm.

Nusrat tried on the earrings. Fayyaz pushed back her hair, his eyes brightening with satisfaction, as he watched her face settle into a pleased smile.

It took Afshan by surprise. A surge of bitterness, as familiar as a forgotten doll discovered in the back of a closet. But, as the evening progressed, her resentment slowly dissipated. She knew that fate had been kind to her. She may not have felt the deep joy she had seen on her sister's face, but nor had she experienced devastation like hers.

⸻

Afshan decided to accompany the couple to Bombay on their next trip. The sisters reached Palghar station just in time, with Nusrat carrying a tiffin box with an assortment of delicacies. Fayyaz, who had come directly from the docks, had already boarded the train.

As they left the station, a toddler sitting at the other end of the compartment started crying. He threw his quilt across the aisle. His weary-looking mother, trying to dislodge him from her lap, strained to reach it from her seat.

Nusrat leaned over and picked up the blanket. It was a patchwork quilt made of odds and ends of different materials joined together by kantha stitches in contrasting colours. She handed it to the young woman.

She opened the tiffin box and offered some jelly sweets to the crying toddler. He took a handful, his expression changing to delight as he bit into the sugar-coated sweets.

She recalled travelling with Sabu when he was that age, holding him in her lap, the rocking motion of the train putting him to sleep instantly. Sabu would have turned thirteen the previous week. She tried imagining her son as a teenager, his plump cheeks flattened, his shoulders touching hers, but she couldn't keep his image whole in her mind.

It sometimes felt unsettling to be pregnant again. When she was carrying Sabu, there had been no legacy of grief, only joy. This time, her pregnancy was filled with anticipation but also bittersweet memories.

The train picked up speed and Fayyaz took out his Ibn-e-Safi novel. Glancing at the cover with a woman holding two fingers up and a pained-looking man in a suit, Afshan said, '*Dangerous Corpses*? I have not read this one. Nusrat, look at this! I know it's meant to be blood but doesn't he look like he is spitting paan? Fayyaz Bhai,' she added, 'I didn't know you are a Safi fan, I read his books too.'

'Your Abba was the one who introduced me to Safi. He used to read the Jasoosi Dunya series, remember?'

'Achha, Nusrat, tell Fayyaz Bhai to read aloud, at least the first chapter, so we can all enjoy it.' And, turning to Fayyaz, she said, 'finish the book before I go, so I can take it from you.'

Nusrat made an effort to lift her spirits. 'Yes, read a little, otherwise you may fall asleep before we reach the next station,' she said to Fayyaz with a deliberate brightness.

Fayyaz smiled at her. 'All right, but only if you both agree not to chatter loudly after I finish and, yes, let me sleep even if I snore all the way to Bombay.'

He opened the book and began reading aloud. Hands folded over her stomach, Nusrat let Fayyaz's steady voice, describing the antics of the Ghalib-quoting detective, wash over her as she gazed out at the unfolding landscape.

Acknowledgements

I would like to thank Chiki Sarkar, my editor, friend and driving force. She has always been a source of wisdom and has guided so many writers like me with her deep understanding of the craft of storytelling.

This book is dedicated to my grandmother, whose impact on my life cannot be quantified. 'Jelly Sweets' is based on the stories she told me about her mother and her childhood in Satpati. She also taught me how to knit, crochet and ignore annoying people by pretending to be deaf.

I extend my appreciation to my exceptional tutors at Goldsmiths, particularly Tom Lee and Blake Morrison, who patiently sat with me and provided invaluable, and sometimes contradictory, advice on

Acknowledgements

my work, which also meant that I was free to pick what suited me best.

Special thanks to Arani Sinha, Devangana Ojha, Sohini Biswas and Shyama Warner for their substantial involvement in this book. I must also mention my admiration for Bhavi Mehta's cover design which perfectly captures the subversiveness of the title.

Narayan and Iravati Lavate's widely reported pursuit of euthanasia sparked my curiosity on the subject and Diane Rehm's *When My Time Comes* based on her interviews with terminally ill patients, doctors and ethicists, proved particularly valuable in presenting diverse perspectives on the euthanasia debate.

Neelam Raaj and Rochelle Pinto, thank you for always giving me your astute advice whenever I have needed it.

A shoutout to my 'Scribes in the City' writing group – Bettina von Hase, Zara Khan, Eden Spence for all your precise feedback. I would have been lost in those university corridors without the three of you.

Alongside my grandmother, there is another ghost in this book – Peter Patrao, who was not only my teacher but also Freddie Mercury's. The 'Element Song' and Madhura's work on the strawberry plantations of Panchgani are shaped by my exchanges with New Era's most beloved teacher.

Thank you Akshay, Mom and Rinke for patiently listening to these stories during long drives and miraculously staying awake until the end.

I am deeply grateful to Aarav and Nitara for giving me the room to be all things I can be along with being their mother.

A Note on the Author

Twinkle Khanna is the bestselling author of three books, *Mrs Funnybones*, *Pyjamas Are Forgiving* and *The Legend of Lakshmi Prasad*.